COPY 1

J
Fiction Avi, 1937-
    Shadrach's crossing / by Avi. -- New
York : Pantheon Books, 1983.
    178 p.   bfc 4-6
    SUMMARY: Living on a poor island in
1932, a young boy determines, despite
his family's bitter opposition, to i-
dentify and somehow bring to justice
the liquor smugglers who have been terrorizing the island.
    ISBN 0-394-95816-0 : 10.99 lib.
    1. Smuggling--Fiction. 2. Islands--Fiction.

· · ·**H**uddled around their kitchen table in the darkness, twelve-year-old Shadrach Faherty and his family, like everyone else on Lucker's Island, know what's going on outside: the smugglers are at work. Kinlow and his men are bringing in another shipment of contraband liquor. Nobody on the island likes Kinlow or what he's doing, but Kinlow has frightened the islanders into helping him—or at least staying out of his way.

Except for Shad Faherty. When Kinlow bullies Shad's parents, Shad resolves to do something, anything, to get rid of Kinlow. But no one will help him, even—to Shad's shame and dismay—his parents. If Shad is going to court danger by taking Kinlow on, he'll have to do it alone.

As Shad stalks Kinlow, gathering the evidence that will put him away, the tension builds. And finally Shad finds himself tracking his enemy across the dunes by night, bringing this suspenseful adventure to its stunning resolution.

OTHER BOOKS BY AVI

Snail Tale
No More Magic
Captain Grey
Emily Upham's Revenge
Night Journeys
Encounter at Easton
The History of Helpless Harry
Man From the Sky
A Place Called Ugly
Who Stole *The Wizard of Oz?*
Sometimes I Think I Hear My Name

Shadrach's CROSSING

a novel by AVI

Pantheon Books

· · · *For Fabio Coen*

Copyright © 1983 by Avi Wortis
Jacket illustration © 1983 by Jeanette Adams
All rights reserved under International and
Pan-American Copyright Conventions.
Published in the United States by Pantheon Books,
a division of Random House, Inc., New York,
and simultaneously in Canada by
Random House of Canada Limited, Toronto.
Manufactured in the United States of America
10   9   8   7   6   5   4   3   2   1
First Edition

Library of Congress Cataloging in Publication Data
Avi, 1937– Shadrach's crossing.
Summary: Living on a poor island in 1932,
a young boy determines, despite his family's bitter
opposition, to identify and somehow bring to justice the
liquor smugglers who have been terrorizing the island.
[1. Smuggling—Fiction. 2. Islands—Fiction]
I. Title.
PZ7.A953Sh   1983   [Fic]   82-19008
ISBN 0-394-85816-6   ISBN 0-394-95816-0 (lib. bdg.)

Shadrach's
CROSSING

1

MR. FAHERTY ANNOUNCED THAT NO ONE WAS TO go out after dinner.

"How come?" his son, Shadrach, asked.

"Do as you're told," Mr. Faherty replied, and he set Shad to sort a huge pile of rusty screws and bolts.

Usually, Shad's father went out after dinner to have a smoke with the men on the dock while his mother sat by the door and read. Then Shad and his younger brother, Brian, could do what they wanted.

That night the tense looks on his parents' faces, the

fact that they too were staying inside, allowed Shad to guess what was happening. The smugglers were coming. And when the smugglers came to Lucker's Island, the island belonged to them.

As it grew dark Mrs. Faherty began to read out loud from an old magazine to help pass the time. It was a story about heroic wireless radio operators during sea storms. Ordinarily, Shad would have been spellbound. That night he couldn't keep still. The thick, heavy feel of coming rain made him restless. His fingers were dry, rust-red from plucking at the metal bits. In the middle of his mother's reading, he said, "These aren't worth a thing."

For a moment no one said a word. Then Mr. Faherty said, "Something."

"Not much," Shad declared, shoving the rusty pile away.

"Got any money in your pockets?" his father asked softly.

Shad colored up. "No, sir," he said. "I don't."

"Well," said his father, "I don't either. But I figure something's worth more than nothing. They're worth something."

Shad, frustrated, started to pick at the bits again.

At about nine o'clock the warnings came, raps on front doors along the row of houses, like the ticking of an angry clock. That was the usual way, a single knock on each door, followed by the slap of steps down the wooden walkway.

Hurriedly, Mr. Faherty reached across the table and turned the key of the hurricane lamp. The flaming wick rolled down, sputtered, and went out. Shad took a deep breath. The stale, heavy smell of kerosene hung in the air.

"Mama," whispered Brian, who didn't like the darkness, or the reasons for it, "Mama, they coming now?"

Gently, his mother touched his hand. "Shhh," she said. "Be patient."

Sitting in the dark, Shad tried to stay calm, wondering what was happening outside. He wished he could see the smuggling for himself.

He could picture the island's dock. Just a few paces from their front door it jutted fifty yards into the bay. And he could almost see the fishing fleet, what was left of it, a dozen small, motorized boats. They rubbed against the dock pilings, making scratching sounds that sang of idle emptiness. Other boats, hauled ashore, lay abandoned, sinking on the beaches, drowning beneath the sand. There were plenty of fish in the sea, but no one on land had money to buy them.

About four months before, the smugglers had first come to Lucker's Island, bringing in cases of rum, whisky, gin, slipping past the Coast Guard pickets. It was risky. Very risky. Smugglers who got caught went to jail. Shad's father had warned him that the smugglers carried guns.

But smuggling was worth the risks. Because of Prohibition, liquor was outlawed. Get liquor to the mainland

and you could make real money. And in 1932, because of the Depression, lots of people, like Shad's father, had no money at all.

After the light went out, the first sound to break the silence came from the channel bell. Shad couldn't tell whether the bell had been blown by a freshening wind or jostled by the sweeping swell of a passing boat. It rang only once. Now the silence seemed harder for Shad to bear than it had before.

No longer able to keep still, he got up, scraping his chair.

"Sit down!" his father barked.

Ignoring him, Shad went to the window, pressed his forehead against the cool glass, and looked out. At the far end of the dock a single lamp was lit. In the damp blanket of the night the lamp's glow looked like a ripe, fuzzy peach.

The channel bell rang again. This time its one loud clang was followed by two short strokes. It wasn't a natural sound. Took a hand to ring it that way.

Shad wondered whose hand.

Suddenly the dock light went off. All became shadow.

Shad couldn't stand it anymore. He went to the door and pulled it open, rattling the doorknob. His father, springing up, tried to grab him, but Shad moved too quickly. As he went out he shut the door behind him.

Along the street all of the twelve houses were dark.

Clouds, reaching in with fat fingers, blotted out the stars. Only a thin white edge of moon creased the darkness. The air reeked of sea. The rain was coming closer. All Shad could hear was the licking of the water. Yet he knew that someone was out there, that the smugglers were coming in.

Afraid his parents would come after him, Shad moved through the darkness away from the house, across the space that was the street. His bare feet, shoeless since the weather had turned warm, hardly felt the rock chips or shell shards that lay upon the ground.

He came up against a large wagon, once used for hauling fish. Eyes riveted on the dock, Shad climbed the wagon, using the wheel spokes as rungs.

Gradually, he was able to make out the shape of a boat. Motor cut off, it was gently coasting, slipping through the water, coming closer.

There was a muffled thump as the boat struck the dock. Wooden posts creaked as they shifted with the impact. A surge of waves washed against the shore. Someone sprang from the boat to the dock carrying—Shad was sure—a line to guide the boat in with.

"All fast!"

More sounds. A hatch being slid back. Footsteps. Voices. A sharp curse as someone slipped and hurt himself. Winches grinding. Thumps as cargo hoisted from the hold banged about.

Then, from inland on the island, the wheezing, hacking cough of an old truck. There was only one truck on the island, and that belonged to Mr. Bennett. Every other week it needed repair. It was Shad's father who kept it going. Bennett paid cash, a dollar a job—the only cash the Fahertys saw.

Shad turned to look toward the sound. The truck was coming slowly, its headlamps dull. Thirty feet from the wagon, it stopped.

"Whoa there!" came a command, as if Bennett were reining back a horse. Shad would have known Bennett's voice anywhere. The motor gave an animal-like whinny as it died. The headlights faded out.

"Bennett?" The question came from somewhere on the dock.

"Who else?" came the croaking voice from the truck. "The Coast Guard?"

"Don't be a fool!" someone replied.

"Ah, fool yourself!"

On the boat, a dim light was switched on. Shadowy forms moved around. Shad thought there might be as many as nine at work. Had they all come from the boat, he wondered, or were some of them island people? He couldn't tell.

Each one gathered up a load, a box, and carried it the length of the dock. Shad could just sense that they were stowing the boxes on the truck.

Back and forth the men went until—Shad couldn't be sure—perhaps forty cases had been moved.

"Done!" came a voice as yet another case was dropped onto the truck.

"About time," Bennett's voice muttered.

Two men moved from the truck along the dock, back toward the boat.

"Come on, come on!" It was Bennett's voice again. "We're not done yet, are we? Got to stash the stuff."

The truck's motor burst into life with snarls and back-firings. Some men climbed onto the back. The headlights lit up. Quickly Shad ducked, sure he had not been seen.

The truck moved off. One of the riders lit a cigarette. In the flare, Shad caught a glimpse of his face. He knew the man, a friend of his father's.

There was a voice from the dock: "Let's get out of here."

Shad turned to look that way again.

With a handsome steadiness, the boat's motor began to growl. The running lights flicked on, and the boat swung about. The throttle eased; the motor responded with a satisfying roar. Then it fairly sang with relief as the boat plunged out of the bay, leaving a glimmering wake of bone-white foam. Very quickly the sound dropped to a hum, until once again all was still. Shad turned and watched as the lights of the houses began to bloom on.

It was then that Shad felt, like a blow from a hammer, a hand crash down over his mouth.

2

SHARPLY SWUNG ABOUT, SHAD WAS TOO SHOCKED to do anything, even to cry out. It was Mr. Kinlow, the man who bossed the island smuggling, who had surprised him.

Mr. Kinlow was short, almost doll-like, with a round, puffy face and smooth pink Santa Claus cheeks. His lips were full, his eyes blue and soft. He always wore city clothes—dark jacket, bow tie, white shirt, polished shoes, and an old-fashioned high wing collar that pressed the flesh of his neck.

"What are you doing here?" he asked. He spoke carefully, evenly, with a trace of Southern accent.

Shad had to gulp for breath. "Nothing," he said.

"What were you watching?" demanded Kinlow.

Shad, feeling sick to his stomach, couldn't speak.

"Answer me!"

"The bay," Shad finally said. His mouth was completely dry.

"What did you see?"

Shad kept his eyes down. "Not sure," he said.

Reaching forward, Kinlow snapped a finger against Shad's chin. The painful sting made Shad jerk his head up. "You know what you saw," said Kinlow. "What was it?"

Eyes smarting with tears, Shad said, "A boat."

"Yes?"

"Unloading."

"What was taken off?"

Shad didn't know what to say.

"Now," said Kinlow, "as before, I desire the truth." He reached forward again.

"Liquor," said Shad quickly. "I think it was liquor."

"Do you know that for sure?"

"No, sir. I think it was."

"What happened to it?"

"Old Bennett came with his truck. Some men put it on, drove it away."

"What men?"

"Didn't see, sir," Shad lied.

"Now then," said Kinlow, putting a hand on Shad's shoulder and squeezing until it hurt, "where did they take the spirits?"

"Don't know," said Shad. "I don't."

Though he kept his eyes on Shad, Kinlow released his grip. Shad rubbed the place where Kinlow had held him. It was sore.

"What's your name?" Kinlow asked.

"Shadrach Faherty."

"Then your father would be Frank Faherty. Did he tell you to come out here to spy?"

"No, sir, he didn't. He told me not to. So did my mother."

"They are wiser than you. How old are you?"

"Almost thirteen."

"Almost?"

"Twelve."

Silently, Kinlow considered. Then he said, "You do know, don't you, that you're not to spy?"

"Yes, sir," said Shad, hanging his head.

"When that warning comes, you are expected to stay in your house." With another snap of his fingers Kinlow made Shad look up again. Shad's eyes brimmed with tears. "You know that, do you?" said Kinlow.

"Yes, sir."

"Do you know why?"

"It's not safe to be out, sir."

"That warning, boy, is a kindness, a palpable act of kindness. It's to keep you out of anger's reach. My anger. My reach." He looked searchingly at Shad. Then, with a nod toward the houses, he said, "Go fetch your parents."

Shad stared at him dumbly.

"Do as I tell you."

His stomach feeling as if it had a rock in it, Shad climbed out of the wagon and walked across the street. When he reached the door he looked back, hoping Kinlow would change his mind. But Mr. Kinlow only pointed toward the house, and Shad knew he had no choice. He knocked on the door. His father opened it.

"Mr. Faherty, sir!" called Kinlow from the wagon. "Might I have the kindness of a brief word with you and your wife?"

Mr. Faherty peered into the dark, too surprised to speak.

"It's of some importance. I should be much obliged."

Giving Shad an angry look, Mr. Faherty put a hand on his shoulder and pulled him inside. Mrs. Faherty was still sitting at the table, the magazine before her.

"Mr. Kinlow wants you too," said Shad, his voice ragged.

She rose slowly, her face ashen. Shad's father held the door as she passed. Then he followed, shutting Shad and Brian in.

Shad looked at his brother. Brian was small, a year and a half younger than Shad, with a cap of light hair crowning a quiet, watchful face. Now his hands were clenched tight and he kept looking at Shad with frightened eyes. More than once he sniffled.

Wanting to look out, Shad made a move toward the window.

"Don't!" cried Brian.

Stung, Shad sat in a chair, swiveling around to avoid his brother's accusing look.

They sat unmoving, doing nothing, for what seemed forever before their mother and father returned.

Mrs. Faherty came in, then Mr. Faherty. He closed the door and stood before it as if to prevent anything or anyone from following him in.

Mrs. Faherty went over to the sink and nervously fingered her hair before a small mirror. Then she turned to look at her husband.

Frank Faherty was not a large man, and he looked older than he was, with a body bent like a bow. His hair was thin, receding high on his forehead. At the moment his chin was covered with a stubbly three-day beard. His eyes were dull, his fingers dark with motor grease.

He said nothing, only stood there, breathing deeply.

Shad, his heart pounding, saw how badly shaken both his parents were. He had never seen them so frightened. It made his insides tighten up again.

Speaking carefully, trying to keep his voice under control, Mr. Faherty said, "I've told you both . . . many times . . . that, when we're warned . . . we're . . . not to go out." He took a deep breath.

Shad, finding it too painful to watch, stared at the floor. When, after a moment, he looked up furtively, his father had closed his eyes.

"What did Kinlow say?" asked Shad.

Mr. Faherty only shook his head.

"He won't have us out there while his business goes on," said Shad's mother.

Shad waited for his father to speak.

"When . . ." Shad's father began after a while, "when you're told not to do something . . . you must not do it."

"It's a free country."

"Is that what you told *him*?" asked Mr. Faherty, his voice weak.

Mrs. Faherty turned hastily to Brian. "Get to bed," she said sharply. "Go on."

His lips trembling, Brian pushed himself from the table. With an imploring look at Shad, he went to the back room they shared. After a final peek through the closing door, he shut himself in.

Shad wished he could go too.

For a long while no one said a word. Then his father said, "You know perfectly well what these men do, don't you?"

"Yes, sir."

"They've been using this island . . . using *us* . . . to . . . to do their smuggling." He spoke very slowly, as if each of the words was hard to say. "When he first came," said Mr. Faherty, "people thought he was from the government, coming to help folks. That didn't last long. But then he laid out lots of . . . smart money to get people to help him. Then he told them if they didn't keep helping, he'd use it against them. Now he's paying almost nothing."

"Can't you stop him?" asked Shad.

Mrs. Faherty touched the side of her face with her fingertips as if it pained her. "No," she said.

"Even if they go," said his father, "there'll be others. Always are. You can be sure of one thing—this Kinlow, there's someone more powerful than he is. He has his boss. God almighty has his boss."

"Can't you do *anything*?"

"If the Coast Guard can't . . ." said Mr. Faherty, but he didn't finish the thought.

"Maybe they *won't*," suggested Shad. "Maybe they're in it too."

Mr. Faherty shook his head.

"You're just making excuses," Shad burst out. "You both are."

"In time," his father said quietly, "they'll go. Meanwhile, don't you cross them."

"I hate Kinlow!" cried Shad. "I hate him!"

"It doesn't matter who you hate," returned his father, his face flushed. "You keep away from Kinlow and what he's doing. That man sees everything. And if he doesn't see, those two men, those bodyguards of his, they'll see. You know what he did? He showed us his pistol. His *gun*, Shad. Do you hear me? He threatened you!"

"Please," said Mrs. Faherty to Shad. "We don't want any trouble."

"You cross him," said Mr. Faherty, "and I hear of it, by God, I'll take that strap in there—" he pointed toward the boys' room—"and give you a whipping that'll bleed your soul."

Shad hung his head.

"Now," said Mrs. Faherty, "now, do you understand?"

"Like . . . slaves," said Shad.

Mr. Faherty turned away. "We will . . . we *all* will . . . do what we're told." He gazed at Shad. "All of us. You understand?"

"Yes, sir," said Shad, feeling shame.

"Go to bed, then," his mother whispered.

Without another word or look, Shad went.

3

As soon as Shad shut the door he heard a muffled sob from his mother, followed by his father's soft murmur. For a moment Shad stood by the door. He hurt inside in ways he had never hurt before.

Brian, already in the bed they shared, had drawn the blanket up over his head. Now he pulled it down under his chin. "What happened?" he whispered.

"Nothing," said Shad, throwing himself on the bed.

"He going to give you a whipping?"

"No."

"Did that Kinlow hurt you?"

"No."

"He hurt Ma? Dad?"

"No. Get to sleep."

For a while Brian kept still. Then he said, "Shad?"

"What?"

"You shouldn't have gone. Shouldn't have."

"It's a free country," said Shad. He turned over, his back toward Brian.

"Shad?"

"*What?*"

"I don't want you to get hurt either."

"I told you, get to sleep!"

Shad stared into the darkness, trying to understand what had happened. It didn't matter so much that Kinlow had treated him that way. Sometimes grown-ups acted that way toward kids. He was used to it. He could handle it. But Kinlow had done it to his parents. And they had let him! They just took it! *Why?* It was so awful he felt sick just thinking about it, and the waves of sickness wouldn't go away.

In his head, Shad invented ways to punish Kinlow: shoot him with his own gun, knock him out, make him get on his knees and crawl, make him go away, put him in jail . . . each notion was more fantastical than the next.

At last, too restless to sleep, too upset, Shad sat up, swung his legs over the edge of the bed, and touched his feet to the floor. "You sleeping?" he said to Brian.

Brian didn't answer.

Quietly Shad stood up. He went to the other side of the room and eased up the window. Chilly, damp air flowed in. The next moment Shad had climbed out and was running down the alley toward Front Street.

The twelve houses on Front Street were gray, broken, built of wood, patched with tar paper, roofed with tin. None had more than four rooms. A few contained what had once been businesses. Mr. Faherty, for instance, had his engine shop in a back room. Davey, Shad's best (and only) friend, lived in a house that contained the island's boat goods store. Shad ran there now.

He sped around to the back of the house, to Davey's window. He shoved up the sash and leaned inside. "Sssst! Davey!"

Davey woke slowly. "What is it?" he grumbled.

"Me, Shad."

"What's going on?"

"Got to talk."

"Time is it?"

"Late."

Sleepily, Davey worked his way out of bed, crawled through the window, and dropped heavily to the ground. In his loose-fitting, light-colored pajamas, he seemed like a half-filled balloon.

"Come on," urged Shad.

"Where?"

"The house."

"The house" was an abandoned three-room house fifty

yards behind Front Street. The people who had lived there—the Tompkins family—had left a year before. Shad remembered how Michael Tompkins, who was fifteen, had cried. No one knew where they had gone, or what had happened to them since they'd left. When people left Lucker's Island they weren't heard from again.

The house had stayed empty. Old wallpaper curled from walls. Floorboards had begun to twist and lift. Only a few windows remained intact. The front room, as if it were the bottom of an hourglass, had started to fill with sand.

Six months after the Tompkinses had gone, Shad and Davey had begun to use the house.

Shad fetched their matches and candle from under the floorboard where they were kept along with the two boxes of crackers and the can of sardines. Shad lit the candle and set it in a handleless cup. The candle glow wrapped them in.

"This better be good," said Davey, yawning widely. He sat back against a pillow that leaked yellowing fluff.

"Guess what?" said Shad.

"Come on . . ."

"I went out and watched Kinlow."

Davey's eyes opened wide. "You didn't!"

"Did. Saw the whole thing, too. Saw the boat coming in with a whole bunch of people. I saw Mr. Markham. Then Mr. Kinlow caught me. I really got scared. And with his finger, just his finger, he hurt me. Kept asking me what I saw."

"You tell him?"

"Not everything. Then he called my parents out."

"Your parents!"

"He threatened them too."

"What'd they do?"

Shad lowered his voice. "My father said I wasn't to mess with him. Said he'd do something if I did." The words were difficult to speak.

"Do something like what?" Davey wanted to know.

"Give me a whipping."

"That Kinlow messed up Mr. Adams," Davey said. "Said he was spying, remember? Beat him up and broke his leg. Mr. Adams went away after that. My ma says he'll never come back. . . . How much they bring in tonight?" asked Davey.

Shad shrugged. "Figure forty, fifty cases."

Davey made a sucking sound. "Lot of money . . . wish I had some." He closed his eyes, the better to imagine it. "Where'd they put it?"

"On Bennett's truck."

"Figures. I always hear the engine. Then what?"

Shad shrugged. "Don't know."

For a moment there was silence. Then Shad suddenly said, "If Kinlow asked you to, would you help him?"

"He wouldn't ask."

"But if he did . . . ?"

"A lot of people help him," said Davey. "Your dad fixes up Bennett's truck. That's Kinlow's money, isn't it?"

Shad said nothing.

"My dad says people have to live," said Davey. "There's no money *anywhere*. Nothing else to do. You would."

"Not me. Not for a million."

"Afraid you'd get caught?" asked Davey.

Shad shook his head.

"Don't worry," said Davey. "The Coast Guard will get them."

"Coast Guard's probably with Kinlow too."

"What makes you say that?"

"They haven't caught them, have they?" said Shad. "Everybody knows what Kinlow's doing. They go out past the twelve-mile limit, meet some English or French boat, buy the liquor, bring it here, store it someplace, and then take it over to the mainland on Mr. Jefferson's ferry. People know. Just, no one wants to *do* anything about it. . . . Look here," Shad continued, "if I could figure out how to get him . . . would you help?"

"People say Kinlow would as soon kill a person as not." Davey looked at Shad, but Shad didn't say anything. "Well?" he demanded.

"I'm going to," said Shad after a moment.

"Going to what?"

"Find a way to get Kinlow."

"What about . . . you know . . . what your dad said he'd do to you, that whipping . . . or what he said Kinlow might do?"

"If I got Kinlow put in jail, I bet I wouldn't get a

whipping. People would be glad. They would—" He stopped abruptly.

"What is it?" asked Davey, alarmed.

Instead of answering, Shad slapped out the candle with his hand.

"What is it?" Davey repeated.

"Someone's outside," Shad whispered.

4

THEY KEPT STILL.

A slight shifting sound came from outside. Shad crawled toward the front door, which hung from the doorframe by one hinge. Rising to his knees, he peered around the door.

Nothing.

He grabbed hold of the door handle and pulled himself up. Davey, breathing hard, had crawled up behind Shad. He tried to stand, but instead he stumbled over a broken floorboard. As he slipped, he fell against Shad and they both crashed against the wall.

Shad could hear the person outside spring up and begin to run away. He struggled to his feet, but his legs were tangled with Davey's. "Get off!" he cried. It took long seconds for them to break apart. When Shad was able to look out again all he saw was a glimpse of white whirling toward the Front Street houses. He tried to follow. Davey struggled to keep up. But when they reached the walkway and looked up and down, no one was there.

"Who was it?" whispered Davey.

"Don't know." Shad's alarm had become puzzlement.

"You see him at all?" asked Davey.

"Wasn't so big."

"One of Kinlow's men is short."

Shad looked toward the beach. It was deserted.

"I bet he heard what you were saying," said Davey. "You know . . . about Kinlow . . . and all."

"So what?"

"Maybe," said Davey, "maybe we shouldn't fool with these guys. If Kinlow finds out what you were saying, he'll get angry."

Shad looked at Davey, disappointed in him. Davey wouldn't return the look. "Let him," said Shad, and he began to walk away. "I'm going to do what I want."

"Where you going?" Davey called.

"Don't know."

Davey started to follow. Then he stopped. "See you tomorrow," he called out.

Without answering, Shad kept going. Only when he reached the beach did he turn around. His friend had gone. For a moment he thought about going home. He decided not to. He really had to think things out.

On the beach Shad sat down on an old log and pulled up his knees and hugged them tightly. A thin mist, thin as any whisper, the first of the rain, began to settle.

Shad wondered who had been listening, and how much he had heard. What would happen? If his parents were told . . . or Kinlow . . . A rush of hatred flowed through him just at the thought of Kinlow. It was Kinlow who was making things so bad. Not just for him, but for everybody. Even Davey was scared of him!

Everybody was.

Agitated, Shad jumped up and walked to the water's edge. Small waves rolled.

Not far from where he was, the dock stood on its wooden pilings, looking like a giant centipede with stiff legs. Idle boats creaked. The light at the end of the dock was on again. Shad wondered who had put it on. A sea gull, perched on one of the taller pilings, slept.

Shad climbed onto the dock and walked to the far end, then sat with his feet dangling. The mist grew thicker, heavier, wetter.

Shad wanted to do something. He could feel the wanting like a solid thing inside him. If nobody did anything about Kinlow, wouldn't things only get worse? But what could he do?

The soft murmur of a motor out in the bay caught his ear. It throbbed sporadically, with a slight sputter, suggesting something wrong.

The gull woke, stretched its wings, but didn't fly. Instead, it cocked its head and watched. Shad wondered if the smugglers were coming back.

His first thought was to get away. Then his angry stubbornness took over. "Free country," he muttered to himself, and waited to see what would happen.

A few moments later the motor out in the bay cut off. Shad stared hard into the darkness but saw nothing, not even a running light.

A splash.

An anchor, thought Shad. But after that, there was only silence again.

He was about to give up, go home, when he heard the soft strokes of oars in water. They came regularly, ten or twelve quiet splashes, followed by a pause. It was as if the rower needed to determine whether he was going the right way.

The sound of oars grew louder. Gradually, out of the almost-rain, a small boat, a skiff, appeared. The rower's back was toward Shad, his yellow slicker glistening. Now and again he would stop and look over his shoulder to see where he was going. As if being jerked along on a string, the skiff moved into the circle of light made by the dock lamp.

With a flap of wings that made Shad jump, the gull leaped into the air, shrieked, and flew away.

Deftly, the man spun the skiff about and faced the dock. Shad, standing up, studied him. It was no one he had ever seen before.

The boat was small and painted white. Its stern bore a name, *The Vole,* in gold letters. Beneath that it read, "Greenport, N.Y."

It was unusual enough for an outsider to come to Lucker's Island. For a stranger to come in the middle of the night was extraordinary.

With delicate touches of oar tips to water, the man kept the skiff some distance from the dock, just on the edges of the light. When the oars lifted, they dripped.

"What's the name of this place?" the man called out. His face was well tanned, and he had a pencil-thin mustache.

"Lucker's Island," returned Shad.

"Glad it's someplace," said the man. "I've got my boat out there—" he gestured with his head—"with motor trouble. It looked like heavy rain and I wasn't sure where I was. When I saw your light I thought to run in. Hoped it was the mainland. An island, you say."

"Mainland's two miles over past the marshes."

"Can I get through?"

"I wouldn't try," said Shad.

"I can get around, can't I?" the man asked. "How far would that be?"

"About five miles."

The man considered that. Then he said, "Seems like you're the only one awake."

"Yes, sir."

"It is late, I suppose," said the man. He looked uncertain what to do. "No electricity here?" he asked, touching his oars to the water's surface to keep his place.

"No, sir."

"Telephones?"

"No, sir."

The man's shoulders seemed to sag. "My luck! . . . How many people actually live here?"

"About forty now. Used to be more."

"Where'd the rest go?"

"Hard times," said Shad.

"Isn't that the truth," said the man. Shad wondered if he cared. The boat, the well-tanned face, the accent— which sounded fancy to Shad—made the stranger seem like money.

"Look here," said the man, "I'll be needing work done on this boat of mine. The motor, anyway. I don't suppose you know anyone here who's handy that way? You do have motors, don't you?"

"My dad fixes them. Does a good job, too."

The man smiled. "By Jupiter, you don't know how pleased I am to hear that. I don't know much about these things. What's his name?"

"Faherty, sir."

"He'll earn himself some money if he can fix it," he said. "You do have money here, don't you?"

"Not much," said Shad seriously.

"What's your name?"

"Shadrach."

The man repeated it, as if to fix it in his mind, even as he edged a little closer to the dock. "I'm sort of new to boats," he explained. "Not used to them at all. Insurance is my line. Regular landlubber, you might say. So I need all the help I can get. Tell you what; I'll come by in the morning if the weather clears. Think I could do that?"

"Yes, sir, you could."

"I suppose you can't live far."

"Fourth house in the row, right by the dock," said Shad.

"And my name is Nevill," said the man. "Austin Nevill." So saying, he lowered his oars and pulled the skiff out of the light.

For a long while Shad stayed at the end of the dock, staring into the bay, listening to the sound of Mr. Nevill's oars. Only when he could no longer hear them did he turn for home. As he did, he yawned.

He got back into his room the same way he had left it, through the open window. As he crawled in, he thought for a moment that he had waked Brian. But Brian only rolled over, pulling the blanket over his white shift. He said nothing.

Shad slipped off his damp clothes and left them on the floor. Suddenly shivering, he crawled under the blanket and drew it over his head. His own breath and body made him feel warm and dim. His thoughts drifted.

What can I do? he kept asking himself. What can I do?

Outside, the rain began to come down hard, bursting against their tin roof like marbles dumped from a bag.

If I don't do something, Shad told himself, there won't be anything or anyone left on the island. "Nothing," he said out loud to himself.

It made him think of what his father had said earlier: "Something's worth more than nothing."

Find a way, Shad kept repeating until the words mingled with the pounding rain. *Find a way ... find a way. . . .*

5

NEXT MORNING SHAD OVERSLEPT. BRIAN WOKE him by standing over the bed and calling, "Lazy bug, lazy bug," again and again.

"What time is it?" Shad asked.

"Past getting up," said Brian. "Ma needs water. She's doing laundry." The Fahertys' water came from a back-yard pump.

Shad, stretching, thought over what had happened the night before. Then he looked at Brian. He was watching Shad intently, a slight frown on his face. "I can help," he suddenly said.

Shad reached out and mussed his brother's hair. "Sure," he told him. "The water's heavy."

"Guess what," said Brian. "Dad's got work. A man came this morning and said his motor needed fixing. He was all dressed in white. Even his shoes. And he's rich. He gave a lot of money to Dad. Ma put it in the bread box." He whispered the last sentence.

Shad wondered what Mr. Nevill might have said about his being out on the dock.

"You going to pump water?" asked Brian. Shad got up.

With Brian's help, Shad brought two full buckets into the house. The moment Shad stepped into the front room he felt the heat coming from the wood stove. Mrs. Faherty placed the large tin washtub on top of the stove, and Shad poured in the water.

"You're up late," she said, wiping away the sweat that rolled down her face.

Without answering, Shad picked up the buckets and started for the door.

"You were told to stay in your room."

Shad stopped, waiting to hear what else she would say. Brian looked on.

"Don't you have anything to say for yourself?" asked Mrs. Faherty.

Shad wondered how she knew he had been out. Had the person who had been listening to him talk with Davey told her, or had it just been Mr. Nevill? He waited and watched her carefully.

She was younger than his father, but looked older. Her

mouth was thin and tight, as was her body. Her teeth were poor, her hair streaked with gray, her arms and hands covered with freckles. The dress she wore, once brightly checked in red and blue, had faded so much that only a vague pattern of lines could be seen.

"A Mr. Nevill was here this morning," she said. "Did Brian tell you? Wanted his motor fixed. He asked for your father by name. He said you were out on the dock last night and you told him he could come by."

"Lucky I was there," said Shad, feeling nervous. What did she know? "I got some work. We don't have to take all our money from Kinlow, do we?"

With a sigh, Mrs. Faherty turned away. "Your dad told you to stay in, and he gave you a warning."

"Yes, ma'am," said Shad, the tension easing. She hadn't said anything about what he had said to Davey, so he was sure she didn't know. Feeling relieved, he went out with Brian to get some more water.

The tub filled, extra pails of water handy, Mrs. Faherty offered Shad breakfast: cold boiled fish and a piece of bread. He ate hungrily.

"What kind of job did that man want done?" Shad asked, finishing up his food.

"Didn't say exactly. Your dad's out on his boat now. But don't you go messing," she warned. "You're looking at something like trouble as is. He's going to speak to you."

Shad decided it would be better if he didn't stay around. He washed his plate, put it away, then started out.

"Can I go with you?" asked Brian. His eyes pleaded. There were almost no children left on the island. None Brian's age. But Shad didn't like it when Brian always tagged after him. It made him feel younger.

"I'll be back soon," Shad told him. "Then we'll play." But when Shad got out in front of the house, Brian had followed.

"Go on," Shad scolded. "Get!"

Sadly, Brian turned back.

Shad walked across the street, stopping at the high water line to study the day. After last night's rain, hardly a cloud was in the sky. It was warm. The beach was smooth. A few gulls strutted, looking self-important, their turned-down beaks giving them a look of smugness. Elsewhere, a pair of sandpipers, stiff-legged, ran up and down, poking their bills into the wet sand, playing tag with waves. Over on the dock some men were sitting. There was no work, but they came every day, stuffing their boredom with empty talk. Some fished.

Nearby, idle boats lay still. Out on the bay, Mr. Nevill's big boat, its skiff attached, rested pretty. On the stern of the big boat, the bold letters, *The Vole—Greenport, N.Y.*, seemed to glitter.

The Vole looked to be about sixty feet in length, painted cream white with gold trim. Its cabin was varnished teak that glistened in the sun. A fancy boat, thought Shad, a rich man's boat. He would have liked to see it up close. If he'd been up earlier, he thought, his dad might have taken him. Depended on how mad his father was at him.

The wheeze and cough of Bennett's truck filled the air. The truck came to a stop not far from where Shad was standing.

As Shad watched, old Bennett climbed laboriously down from the open cab and lifted the hinged motor hood. Shad wondered if Bennett was going to ask his father to do a job on the truck. Two motors to fix—Nevill's and Bennett's—would mean a lot of money.

"Hey, boy." Bennett motioned to Shad. "Come here."

Shad walked over.

"Where's your father?" the old man demanded in a loud, raspy voice. He had shaggy, mussed hair, bushy eyebrows, and a thick mustache stained with tobacco. Mrs. Faherty said he drank.

"He's out there," said Shad, pointing to *The Vole.* "A man came in last night with motor trouble. Couldn't make it to the mainland."

The men on the dock—Shad knew them all—looked up. They had been listening.

Bennett, making a half turn, studied *The Vole.* "Rich sailor," he said sarcastically. Then he turned back to the truck.

"Need my dad's help?" asked Shad hopefully.

"Keep looking at the motor," said Bennett, his voice suddenly low.

"What?"

"I want those dock loafers to think I'm talking about this motor, fool. They don't have to hear what I'm saying. Just you."

"Yes, sir," said Shad, bewildered.

"And keep your mouth shut. And listen with your head, not just your ears. Kinlow says you were out spying on him last night."

"Just watching."

"He says *spying*, and what he says goes around here. You understand? Don't mix with him or his two pals. Don't fool with them at all! Your father's a pal of mine. Do you get me? Now, you move off like I said nothing. Go on!" He reached up and pulled the hood down with a bang.

The men on the dock were watching.

"I said move, boy!" shouted Bennett. "Move!" He climbed back into his truck and set the motor going with a symphony of snorts. The truck lurched ponderously away, leaving Shad to look after it.

The whole world seemed to know what he had done. Is that good or bad? he asked himself. . . . If he tried to do something about Kinlow, would anyone help?

Shad didn't break from his thoughts until he realized that Brian was standing right in front of him. He was looking up, staring at Shad, a puzzled look on his face.

"Ma wants you," he said.

"I'm coming," said Shad. Slowly, he began to walk back toward their house. Brian followed, half a step behind.

* * *

"I'd like you to go cross-island to Mr. Jefferson's ferry," said Mrs. Faherty. "Tell him to hold places for me next Tuesday. Over and back."

Going to the mainland was always a special occasion. Shad guessed this trip was because of Mr. Nevill's money. There were so many things they needed, and they barely had enough money for food.

"Can I go too?" Shad asked.

"We'll see," said his mother. "Depends on your behaving."

"I'm going," announced Brian.

Shad felt stung that his brother had been promised a trip, while he hadn't. But he was too proud to beg, and left the house to do as his mother asked.

Lucker's Island, while three miles long, was only a mile and a half at its widest. The firm beach ran like a ring around it. The middle of the island consisted of rolling, sandy dunes, with low, wind-cut scrub pine bushes and patches of coarse grass. Here and there were piles of stones, and at the southern end, stretches of pebbles. But mostly it was sand.

Sometimes, during bad storms, the whole island seemed to disappear. During the last hurricane, it almost had. Houses had been blown flat, as though pressed by hands.

There was no real road on the island. Bennett's truck went around its edges, on beaches where the sand was firm. To get around on foot, there were paths that crisscrossed the dunes.

The path that Shad took twisted like a snake, connecting one house to another. Most of the houses were abandoned. It always amazed Shad how quickly, how quietly, the empty houses fell apart. First the windows went. Then the doors. Roofs sagged. Walls shrank, split, turned colorless as they caved in. The only thing left behind was silence. Shad wondered, as he always did, where the people who had lived in the houses had gone. Were they better off somewhere else?

But if, as his mother had told him, the whole world had gone to poor, why did people bother to leave? What was the point of going if every place was as tired, as poor, as Lucker's Island?

Would *he* ever leave? Or would he stay forever, stay till he was a man? What would be left by then?

Would Kinlow still be there?

Kinlow. Shad felt as if nothing in his life would change unless Kinlow left the island for good.

Shad veered off the path and climbed to the top of a dune. From its soft peak, standing ankle-deep in fine sand, he surveyed the island, his world. He looked across the marsh, toward the mainland. The mainland seemed distant and immense, a foreign country. So huge. So full of people. And modern. Cars. Electricity. Radio. Motion pictures that talked. Shad wondered what it would be like to live there. He wished he could go and find out.

He looked back toward the bay. On *The Vole,* two people came out of the cabin, then climbed into the skiff. It was Mr. Nevill and his dad.

Shad looked northward. Twenty or so houses lay scattered. Empty. Still. Broken.

Except for one house. It was the house where Kinlow stayed when he was on the island. Though Kinlow only came on Sundays and left Tuesdays, people always avoided the area.

Kinlow's house wasn't a new one. But it wasn't broken-down, either. It did have a new chain link fence around it. Inside the fence were a table, chairs, and a flagpole. A green streamer hung limply from the pole. Shad wondered what kind of flag it was.

As Shad looked, a man came out of the house. He stood for a moment, one hand on the doorframe, the other shading his eyes. It was one of Kinlow's two bodyguards.

Realizing he was standing right in the open, Shad dropped flat. Chin resting on the backs of his hands, he kept watching.

Kinlow's man went back into the house. The next moment he returned, a red cloth hanging from his arm. He went to the flagpole and hauled down the green streamer, leaving it to lie on the ground. Then he hooked up the red flag. It hung as limply as the first.

Two others came out of the house. Shad recognized one of them as Kinlow and wondered if he was carrying his pistol. The second man carried a box with what looked like a net attached to its top.

The man carried the box to the table. Then he took from it some device which he settled onto his head. Kinlow took a watch from his pocket and looked at it.

Shad began to understand what was happening. The net-like thing on the box was an antenna. On the man's head, earphones. It was a radio they had set up. Shad had seen pictures of one in a magazine.

Shad looked across the island toward the bay. While he had been watching Kinlow, Nevill had brought his father to shore. Now, Nevill was returning to *The Vole*. Halfway there, he stopped rowing. He took something from his pocket—the same gesture Kinlow had made with his watch—and then began to row again, much faster than before.

Suddenly Shad remembered something. The night before Mr. Nevill had told him he knew nothing of boats. Yet he had handled the skiff as if he'd been around boats from the day he was born. And right now he was making that skiff fly. Whatever he was, he wasn't a landlubber.

Who was he?

Shad looked back toward Kinlow's house. The radio operator was talking to Kinlow. Kinlow answered. Then the man began to jiggle his hand over the key. He was sending a message.

Neville reached *The Vole*, and sprang aboard. He ran into his cabin only to return, a spyglass in his hand. He held it to an eye, aiming at the island. Moments later he darted back into the cabin.

Kinlow's man worked the key.

It was then that Shad made the connection between the things he had just seen. The red flag was a signal that Mr. Kinlow was sending a message.

And it looked as if he was sending that message to Mr. Nevill!

6

SHAD LAY ON HIS STOMACH, EYES SHIFTING FROM Kinlow's house to *The Vole* and back.

The man working the radio stopped. He pulled off the earphones, picked up the machine, and then followed Kinlow into the house. The third man lowered the red flag but didn't run up the green. Instead, he took both flags inside.

Out on the bay, Mr. Nevill had stepped from his cabin and was standing on the deck of his boat, hands on his hips, looking. Shad would have sworn he was looking right at Kinlow's house. Then Nevill wheeled about, returned to the cabin, and did not come back out.

Just when Shad was certain nothing else would happen, the door to Kinlow's house opened again. Out came Kinlow and his friends. One of them was carrying a satchel. The other locked the front door. Then the three set out along a path, away from Shad.

At first Shad thought they were going to meet Mr. Nevill. Soon it became clear that they were going the other way, toward the island's marsh side. Shad followed.

It was easy enough to track them. The dunes were high, the valleys between them low—Shad could keep out of sight easily. And it wasn't long before Shad knew exactly where the three were going: the same place as he—the landing spot for Mr. Jefferson's marsh ferry.

The marsh that separated Lucker's Island from the mainland town of Millford was two miles wide, an ever-shifting maze of shallow, brackish water laid over oozing, blackened slime. Thousands of small, humpbacked salt-hay islands broke the surface.

At full moon—when the tide ran extra low—a tall person *might* get across the marsh on foot if he knew the way and didn't mind the stinking muck. But at high tide not a dry spot could be found. With every step a walker took, he would sink to his knees, or farther.

People crossed to the mainland in boats, or took the ferry.

Staying behind Kinlow and his friends, Shad watched as they came down from the dune that bordered the beach. From his high place, Shad could see Mr. Jefferson's ferry, a large, square, flat-bottomed boat with a paddle wheel rigged to its stern. It was churning slowly toward the island.

Mr. Jefferson, an old, knobby man who reminded Shad of a rooster without feathers, had built the boat himself, using a lot of bicycle parts. He sat upon a bicycle seat, steered with bike handlebars, drove the paddle wheel with a long link chain.

As Shad watched, the ferry ran up to the shore.

Shad knew he had a perfect right to go down and deliver his mother's message. But he didn't want to go anywhere near Kinlow. Staying where he was, he watched as a passenger got off.

Shad recognized the passenger as Mr. Sheraton. Mr. Sheraton spoke briefly to Mr. Jefferson, appeared to exchange a few words with Kinlow, and then set off down the beach, knapsack on his back.

Kinlow climbed on the ferry, and his two friends pushed it back into the water. Mr. Jefferson, high on his seat, began to pedal. As the wheel behind foamed and fussed, the boat backed deeper, turned, then started through the marsh.

Shad realized that Kinlow was leaving one day earlier than he usually did. And the morning after Nevill came! It seemed as if there had to be a connection, but Shad couldn't be sure.

Frustrated, Shad knew he had to wait. The trip to the mainland took forty-five minutes each way. Thinking to kill the time, he decided to follow after Mr. Sheraton.

* * *

Mr. Sheraton had been coming to Lucker's Island for almost six months. He was of middle age, with jet-black hair that continually flopped down over his eyes. He often threw his head back to flip the hair away. His face was slack, the skin loose beneath his chin. The blue suit that he wore was baggy, and his shoes were made of cloth.

Twice a week he appeared, often—but not always—on Tuesdays and Saturdays, to check a rain gauge that had been set up on the island's barren southern point. A box had been placed there on stilts four feet off the ground. On one side of the box was a door. It carried a sign:

WARNING: U.S. GOVERNMENT PROPERTY
KEEP OUT!

Davey's father had told Shad and Davey that inside the box was nothing more than a cup. Through a hole in the top of the box, rainwater fell into the cup. What Mr. Sheraton did was measure how much water came into the cup and write it down in a little book.

It certainly appeared that Mr. Sheraton was off to do his measuring now. Shad, glad to be doing something that was only fun, trailed Sheraton right to the box, certain that he wasn't revealing himself.

When Mr. Sheraton reached the box, he opened it. He took a ruler and a small book from his knapsack, did something in the box—Shad couldn't see what—and then wrote in the book. That done, he shut the door and put book and ruler away in his knapsack.

The notion that this was the man's whole job, that he got money for doing such a thing, made Shad want to laugh. There was nothing to it!

Mr. Sheraton, his job done, turned around slowly. Instantly Shad dropped to the ground, not certain himself why he took the trouble to hide.

When Shad raised his head, Sheraton was looking out over the water. He seemed to be watching the bay with particular interest.

Then Sheraton began to walk down the island's middle, over the dunes. At the top of each one he'd stop, look about, then go on. Once, he paused. From his knapsack, he took a pair of binoculars, and with them he searched a wide arc.

Every time he thought Sheraton was going to turn his way, Shad ducked. But when he got up again after the fifth time, ready to go on, Mr. Sheraton was nowhere in sight.

Taken completely by surprise, Shad looked in all directions. The man had simply disappeared.

Shad climbed the next dune and searched again. There was still no sign. It was so odd for Sheraton to be there one moment, and not there the next. Shad began to wonder if the man had noticed him. Then he told himself that it didn't matter if he had. Why should Mr. Sheraton care who watched him? Anyway, Shad told himself, Mr. Sheraton had probably just taken a different way back to the ferry. It didn't matter.

He thought about the government box. There was nothing else like it on the island. It had only been there for a few months. Why, Shad wondered, had it even been put there? Did it mean there was something special about the island?

Shad decided to investigate the box. He headed back toward it, though, still a little cautious, he kept an eye out for Sheraton. Just in case.

When he came close to the box he examined it carefully, then, once again, gazed about for Sheraton. The man was nowhere in sight. Shad turned back to the box. It was so hard to believe that what he'd seen Sheraton do was the whole job. Maybe there *was* something else.

He lifted his hand to the knob on the box door, trying to pay no mind to the warning sign. Then he paused, took one final look about, and pulled at the knob. The door sprang open.

"Please, you must not do that."

Shad spun about. Right behind him was Mr. Sheraton.

"Good afternoon," Sheraton said formally. He came forward and shoved the box door shut with a click. Shad stood there completely tongue-tied. "Were you looking for me?" asked Sheraton, smiling.

Shad shook his head. He felt stupid and embarrassed.

"Two can play hide and seek, you know," Sheraton said. "Interested in my work?"

"Yes, sir," said Shad, almost afraid to lift his eyes.

"Find what you were searching for?"

"Just curious," Shad managed to say.

"What did you learn?"

Shad shrugged. "Nothing."

"The sign does say you're not to touch it. It's the property of the government, the United States government."

"Yes, sir."

Mr. Sheraton pulled the door open and pointed to the cup. "If you disturbed anything in there, my reading would be useless."

"Yes, sir."

"You didn't do any harm this time. But you do understand what I've said?"

Shad nodded. He wished he could just go away.

Sheraton, however, kept him there with a long gaze. "Do you have a name?"

"You going to tell my parents?" asked Shad, suddenly alarmed.

"Not if you promise to keep your hands off this box. Do I have that promise?"

"Yes, sir."

"Good. Now, what's your name?"

"Shadrach Faherty."

Sheraton smiled and shrugged off his knapsack. Kneeling, he took out his little book and wrote something in it. "Your name," he explained. "I'm not good at remembering things."

Shad understood the gesture. It was a warning that Sheraton *would* remember him. But then Mr. Sheraton took out his binoculars. "No hard feelings," he said, and held up the binoculars. "Care to have a look?"

Shad wanted to hold them. They did seem splendid, bound in black leather, with shiny brass metal bands.

"Try them," said Sheraton.

Cautiously Shad reached out and took them, then put them to his eyes. Distant images leaped forward. He looked into town, into his own backyard. When · he turned slightly, *The Vole* loomed large. Even as he watched, Mr. Nevill came out of his cabin and hauled in the skiff. Shad watched as he climbed into the boat and began to row toward shore.

Shad turned toward the marsh. He could see the paddle-ferry churning along.

He handed the binoculars back.

Sheraton took them. "Why were you following me?" he asked.

Shad, feeling embarrassed again, only shrugged. "Just doing it," he admitted.

"I saw you right from the start," said Sheraton, watching Shad carefully. "Did you think I was up to something wrong?"

Shad shook his head.

"You hear talk about smugglers around here. Think that's what I was doing?"

Shad, taken by surprise, stared at Sheraton. "No, sir," he got out. "I didn't."

Sheraton sat down on a rock and toyed with some pebbles. "I suppose people don't actually look like smugglers, do they? But then, maybe they do. Ever see smugglers hereabouts?"

Shad felt increasingly uneasy.

"Well, you might not want to say," Sheraton continued. "People are hard up for money these days. They'll do most anything to get it. I don't suppose you island people talk about such things. Certainly not to a stranger like me."

Shad gazed at him suspiciously, trying to understand what he was after.

"Well," continued Sheraton, "if there are smugglers, I guess the Coast Guard will catch them. Isn't that what they're supposed to do?"

"They won't," Shad blurted out.

"How's that?"

"They don't even try!"

Sheraton flipped the hair out of his eyes. "How do you know? You just guessing? . . . Maybe you don't want them caught."

Sorry he had spoken, Shad pressed his lips together. But as he stared down at his feet a new idea came to him. The measuring of the rainwater that Sheraton did hardly made sense to him. Maybe that wasn't Mr. Sheraton's real job. But Mr. Sheraton *was* a government man. Perhaps he really was working for the government, but trying to help catch the smugglers.

"The Coast Guard would have to catch the smugglers with their stuff, the evidence," said Sheraton. "By surprise. The way I surprised you." He gazed down the island. "Trouble is, on a small place like this it would be hard to surprise anyone. The Coast Guard would need help. What do you think? Think anyone here would be ready to help them?"

Shad said nothing. He was too busy trying to put together his new thoughts.

Sheraton got to his feet. "Still," he said, "the government does give reward money to people who help. Real money." He laughed. "That's why I bring my binoculars. No telling what I might see." He tossed his head, flipping the hair out of his eyes. "Guess I'd better get back to the ferry."

He began to walk away, but after only a few steps he stopped and turned around. "Look here," he said, entirely serious. "I'll make a deal with you. If you *do* see something, why don't you let me know? You can always leave a message in that box of mine. I'll know what to do with it. If I get a reward, I'll share it with you. But I want to know before anyone else. I'm here often enough. What do you say? A deal?"

Shad nodded yes.

"But remember," said Sheraton, "the deal's off unless you tell me *first*."

Again Shad nodded.

"Good boy," said Sheraton. "Just don't get into any trouble." And he began to move away, taking long strides.

Shad, his excitement growing, watched Sheraton go. He no longer felt alone. He *would* be able to do something.

7

SHAD FOLLOWED SHERATON TO THE FERRY LAND-
ing, but openly this time. Just watching Sheraton made
Shad feel better.

When they reached the ferry landing, Sheraton
dropped his knapsack, sat down, and propped himself up
against a rock. Book in hand, he stayed there, reading.

Shad, guessing that Mr. Sheraton didn't want Mr. Jefferson to know they knew each other, kept his distance.

When Mr. Jefferson finally brought his ferry back to
shore, Shad ran forward to meet him.

"My ma says to tell you she wants to go across next Tuesday morning. Back and forth. Says she wants you to hold places."

"Just herself?"

"My brother too."

"What about you?"

"She didn't say."

Mr. Jefferson cocked his head and gave Shad a wink. "Get yourself into trouble?"

Shad, wondering what Mr. Jefferson knew, didn't reply.

"Tell her I'll be going about eight that morning," said Mr. Jefferson.

During the conversation, Sheraton had looked up briefly, but no more. As he got on the boat, Mr. Jefferson suddenly called to Shad. "Hold it," he said. "Tell her I'll be going about ten in the morning or thereabouts." And he began pumping in earnest, and the boat moved away.

Shad stood on the shore and watched the boat go. When it began to cut between the salt-hay islands, he turned away. Taking the same path by which he had come cross-island, he headed back home.

Shad was feeling good. The notion that Mr. Sheraton, a government man, was going to be his friend meant a lot. As Shad saw it, his part was to get evidence, then get it to Mr. Sheraton. He did wonder if he should have told Sheraton the facts he already knew. He began to wish he had.

Reaching the top of a dune, he looked back. The marsh ferry had moved a fair distance. Shad turned the other way. The bay was quiet.

Finally, Shad looked at Kinlow's house.

He stared at it, fascinated. Perhaps that was where they stored the liquor until they were ready to take it to the mainland.

The evidence . . .

If it was . . . if he told Sheraton . . .

Shad kept looking at the house and thinking about how deserted it was. Kinlow and his friends were off the island. Even if they did come right back with Mr. Jefferson—which would be very unusual—they wouldn't get back for another hour or more. There would be plenty of time to search the house.

But Shad didn't move. Instead, he watched the house from where he was, reminding himself that to go into it would be awfully dangerous. Just thinking about it made his heart race. But if he did, and if he found some evidence, and if he told Mr. Sheraton . . .

Nervous, tense, telling himself not to do it, not to play the fool, not to place himself in danger, Shad nevertheless knew he was going to try.

He began to walk toward the house.

When he reached the fence, he leaned against the wire mesh, staring at the building. It nested in a half moon of dunes. Like most of the houses on the island, it was one story, built of wood. An outhouse was in the back. Tin roof. The windows were curtained.

Trying to be casual, Shad moved toward the gate.

Halfway there, he decided against going in that way. It was too open. Someone just might see him. He followed the fence around to the back. As he went, he kept looking about. He saw no one.

He did see a back door.

He studied the fence. It wasn't all that high. Grabbing over his head, poking his toes into the mesh, he began to climb.

In seconds, he reached the top and slung his legs over. Momentarily, he sat there, hands to either side, keeping his balance.

A quick shove and he dropped down inside the fence, his feet hitting the sand hard. In five long strides he had reached the back door.

No longer thinking about the possible consequences of what he was doing, Shad pushed at the door. It wouldn't give. He pushed harder. Still no movement. Then he gave it a shove with his shoulder. The door burst open. Unprepared, he tripped, pitching forward, tumbling down onto his knees.

He was inside Kinlow's house.

He was in a fairly big room that was dingy, stale, and smelled strongly of tobacco. Drawn curtains made the place dim. There were a few chairs, and a table littered with cans of food, some of them open. Ashtrays were full of half-smoked cigarettes. Dirty dishes were in the sink. In one corner of the room lay the red and green flags. The radio equipment sat by the front door. On the back of the door hung a large calendar.

To his left, there was a wall on which were two closed doors. The wall looked newly made.

Slowly, blood still pounding in his ears, Shad got to his feet. He noticed a hook latch on the back door. Thinking he'd feel safer with the door locked, he lifted the hook and dropped it in place.

Feeling bolder, he began to walk about. He checked the front door. It was locked. He stopped and studied the calendar. One day a week was crossed out, and the next Monday, Shad noticed, had a circle drawn around it. Something important was going to happen then, he thought.

He pushed at the closest door. It opened into a small room that contained nothing but three beds, cots really, all unmade. The blankets were a tumbled mess. Ashtrays were full to overflowing. Open girlie magazines lay on the floor.

The second door opened into another small room. It was full of wooden boxes. There were five rows of them, ten stacks to a row, piled six high. A couple of boxes, the lids pried loose, lay apart from the rest.

Shad went into the room and lifted the lid of one of the opened cases. It contained bottles. Shad picked one up. It was green glass with no label. But it was full. Certain that it contained liquor, Shad put it back.

He had found the storage place. *The evidence.*

Carefully, he pushed the box lid down, hoping he had put it back the way it was originally. At that very moment, there was a knocking at the front door of the house.

Shad didn't move. He couldn't. He stood, immobile, aware only of how stupid he had been, how wrong it was for him to be in that room, that house. He shut his eyes. He could hardly breathe.

Again the knocking came.

Knowing he couldn't stay where he was, Shad forced himself to move away from the liquor cases. He stepped back behind the door, hoping that if anyone came in and looked into this room, he wouldn't be seen.

More knocking. A man called, "Anyone home?"

The voice was vaguely familiar, but the few words Shad had heard weren't enough of a clue. He looked to see if there was a way to get out of the room besides the door. There were two windows, but both had been boarded up.

He waited for another knock to come. None did. But as he listened, he heard the caller pushing against the front door, rattling it, trying to get in.

Then there was silence.

On his toes, Shad came out of his hiding place behind the door and peeked into the main room. Empty as he had left it.

All the windows had curtains: no one could look in. For the moment he was safe, but he knew he had to get out of the house, and fast.

Now it was the back door that rattled. Even though he knew he had latched it, Shad felt sweat on his body. He had come that close to being found.

Again there was silence.

Giving the caller time to leave, Shad slowly counted to

a hundred. When he finished, he made himself do it again.

The front door rattled once more. Shad inched his way to the back door, then stood behind it, making himself wait.

Nothing happened. Not a sound.

Reaching out a hand, he flipped the hook latch open. He waited. Then cautiously, he began to pull the door in, peering through the widening crack. He saw nothing. Encouraged, he opened the door all the way and quickly stuck his head out. No one.

The fence was about fifteen feet away. Past the fence, the dunes rose up steeply.

Shad studied the fence, picking his place, right opposite the door. Once more he looked about. Certain no one was there, he braced himself. With a sudden burst, he flung himself out of the house.

He hit the fence and scrambled up, paying no heed to the pain in his right foot as it banged against the fence. He vaulted over the top and came down on the other side, falling on his back.

Winded, but knowing he might still be in danger, Shad made himself get up. He clawed his way up the dune, dove over the top, and rolled wildly down the other side until he hit bottom.

He was safe.

Breathless, Shad lay at the bottom of the sandy valley, heart galloping, lungs pinched, but his fear beginning to ebb.

As he lay there, as his calmness returned, he began to think about who the man who had knocked might be. He wanted to know. That might be evidence, too.

Shad rolled over, scrambled back to the top of the dune, and looked down at the house.

The first thing he saw was that he had left the back door open wide. He could only hope that when Kinlow returned he wouldn't notice, or care. He was not going back to shut it.

Shad couldn't see the front of the house, so he couldn't tell if the caller was still there. If he really wanted to find out—and he did—he would have to circle around.

Dropping back down behind the dune, he ran along the bottom till he was three-quarters of the way around to the front of the house.

Up the dune he crawled, then he crouched behind a clump of thick dune grass. From there he could look at the front of the house with ease.

At first glance the area seemed completely deserted. It took Shad a few moments to realize that a man, back toward him, was sitting by the table.

The man was so quiet, so unmoving, that at first Shad thought he was asleep. Then, as if he knew that Shad wanted to see him, he got up and turned about.

It was Mr. Nevill.

Shad watched, fascinated, trying to understand exactly what Mr. Nevill was doing. That he was doing something *with* Kinlow made the best sense. Pretending he knew nothing about boats, the wireless message, visiting his house—they had to be working together! But there he was, trying the front door again, only to back off. At one point he attempted to look through a curtained window. Failing at that, he started to move around the house.

As he did, Shad pushed himself higher to watch. In the soft sand his hand slipped, sending down a small shower of sand.

Nevill spun about.

Instantly, Shad threw himself down the side of the dune. Without pausing he scrambled up the next and leapt over the top of it. Then once more he looked back, only to see Mr. Nevill moving hurriedly away. He had scared him off!

Shad decided he mustn't stay any longer himself. He headed for home.

8

SHAD WENT FIRST TO HIS OWN HOUSE. BUT AFTER he had told his mother that he had delivered her message to Mr. Jefferson, he didn't stay.

As before, Brian tried to follow him. "Shad!" he called, as Shad hurried out.

"I have to hurry," returned Shad.

"You said you'd play!" Brian reminded him.

"Later."

"Where you going?"

"Davey's."

* * *

Davey was in his parents' store, dusting mostly empty shelves. Davey's father was there, working on a newspaper crossword puzzle.

"Can Davey come out for a minute?" Shad asked from the doorway.

Davey's father looked up. He was big, with an enormous stomach, huge hands, and a dark face. "What's it about?" he asked, studying Shad.

"Nothing."

"Sure?"

"Yes, sir."

Davey's father looked to Davey, then back at Shad, then back to his puzzle. "For a few minutes," he murmured.

The two boys stood outside Davey's house. "What is it?" asked Davey.

"We have to go to our place. I can't tell you here."

"Something happen?"

"You coming?"

Davey looked behind him to see if his father was watching. "Okay," he said.

They went behind the Front Street houses and into their house. Shad sat right down on the floor, back against the wall. Davey, nervous, stood.

"What is it?" Davey demanded.

"You going to sit?"

Reluctantly, Davey sat. Shad, watching him, remembered how his friend had acted the night before. "You don't have to listen, you know."

"I know."

"I was going to give you another chance."

"You going to tell me what's up?" asked Davey.

"Listen to this," said Shad, and he told Davey about everything that had happened from the time they had separated the night before: his meeting with Nevill, Kinlow's flags, the radio message, the connection with *The Vole*. He told Davey about Mr. Sheraton, too. Finally he told about going into Kinlow's house.

Davey listened with increasing ill ease. "Boy," he said when Shad had finished talking. "If Kinlow finds out, he's really going to kill you."

"He's not going to find out. Not unless you tell him."

"Not me!" cried Davey. "Cross my heart! But my father," he warned, "he heard about you and Kinlow and what happened. Mrs. Stevenson told him."

"How'd she know?"

Davey shrugged. "He was asking me about it. Told me not to mess around. You sure this Mr. Nevill didn't see you at the house?"

"I don't think so."

Davey considered. "You really think Mr. Sheraton is a G-man?"

"He works for the government, doesn't he? And he did offer me a reward, sort of. Told me I should bring any evidence I got to him first. What else could he be?"

"I don't know. What are you going to do now?"

"I'm going to get Kinlow in jail."

"Think so?"

"You going to help?" retorted Shad.

"I'm not sure," Davey said after a minute.

"This is your last chance," said Shad. "I won't give you any more."

"I know."

"Scared?"

"Yeah. And you should be too. But that's not the only thing. You—" He stopped suddenly. "What's that?" he asked, his voice dropping low.

Shad had heard it too. Just like the night before. Someone was outside.

This time Shad was prepared. With his hand, he cautioned Davey to keep quiet. Then he waited until another sound came. Meanwhile, he looked around the room. A stick lay not too far off. Stretching carefully, he picked it up and held it like a club.

Davey shrank back.

Suddenly, Shad jumped up, tore out of the house, and leaped around the corner to confront the listener. There, crouched under the window, was Brian.

Brian jumped to his feet and tried to run off. Shad, flinging the stick away, was right after him. He grabbed his brother's arm. Struggling to get free, Brian twisted around and fell to the ground.

"What were you doing?" Shad yelled, not at all sure whether he was more upset or relieved that it was only Brian.

Brian looked up at Shad, his eyes rapidly filling with tears.

"What were you doing?" repeated Shad.

Brian shook his head.

"Was that you last night, too?" demanded Shad. "Was it? You better tell me!"

Brian, too frightened to speak, nodded yes.

"It's none of your business!" shouted Shad.

Davey had come out of the house and was looking on from a few feet away.

"Tell me what you heard!" Shad said.

"What you said."

"All of it?"

"Some."

"What're you going to do about it?"

"I want to help."

"You can't."

"I can too," insisted Brian.

Shad, frustrated, started to walk away.

"I don't like Kinlow either!" Brian cried after him.

Shad swung around. "You going to tell what I said and what I did?"

"Not if you let me help."

"You *can't* help!" cried Shad. "You're a baby! You'll get hurt!"

"I'm *not* a baby. Anyway, you'll get hurt too."

"He better not tell," put in Davey.

"I will," insisted Brian, "'less you let me help."

"Go home, baby," Shad told him. "Go home and mind your own business. We don't need you."

Brian got to his feet and backed off a few steps. His eyes brimmed with tears. "I'm going to tell," he warned.

"If you do . . ." Shad made a fist.

"Don't care!" said Brian. Then he turned and fled, pausing only to shout, "Don't care!"

Shad and Davey watched him go.

"He going to tell?" asked Davey.

"Better not."

"Look," said Davey. "I don't think we should take any chances. He might tell, you know. We're only going to get into trouble."

"He won't tell."

"People know you were messing with Kinlow last night, don't they? You can't hide things around here. You can't."

"I wasn't 'messing.' "

"What if they find out about what you did today?"

Shad looked at Davey, then began to walk away with disgust. "That's okay," he said. "I can do it without you."

Davey ran after him and grabbed his arm. Shad shrugged off his hand and kept going.

"Come on," said Davey. "If all the grown-ups and the Coast Guard can't get Kinlow, how are we going to? And what'll happen if you do get caught? Ever think of that? You shouldn't get mad at me just because I thought about it."

Shad kept walking.

"You don't even know what you're going to do!"

Shad whirled around. "I do!" he shouted. "I've got the whole plan in my head!"

"Yeah, what?"

"What difference does it make to you?" said Shad scornfully. "You're not going to be in on it. You're too scared," he shouted, breaking into a run and refusing to look back.

"You're crazy, Shadrach Faherty," Davey called after him. "Crazy! You're going to get yourself killed!"

9

SHAD RAN A GOOD WAY ALONG THE BEACH BEFORE
he stopped and let himself cool down. Then he turned
back toward home, walking slowly.

He had spoken big to Davey, but he knew it was just
talk. Other than to tell Mr. Sheraton what he'd found in
Kinlow's house and what he thought about Mr. Nevill,
he had no plan. But at least, he reminded himself, that
was *something*.

Halfway home, he decided he'd best talk to Brian
again and warn him to keep quiet. If Brian told, he might

just ruin the little he'd planned. But when Shad got home no one was there.

The house was cool, airy, smelling of strong soap. Shad felt hungry. When he took a piece of bread from the bread box, he saw the pile of dollar bills that Mr. Nevill had paid. It was a lot of money. Maybe ten dollars. Remembering how glad he had been before, thinking it honest money, he felt bitter.

Restless, he went out to the dock. As usual, a few men were sitting about. As he walked by, he felt their eyes on him.

Standing out at the end of the dock, he looked at *The Vole*. As he watched, his father poked his head above the gunwale. When he saw Shad he waved; then he climbed into the skiff and began to row toward shore.

Shad's first thought was to run off, sure his father was only coming to scold him. But as the skiff drew closer, Mr. Faherty called out, "Need your help!"

At the end of the dock was a ladder. Shad climbed down and waited. When the skiff was close enough, he stepped in and pushed off. His father began to row back to *The Vole*.

"Not a bad boat," said Mr. Faherty. "No big thing to fix, either. Plugs are fouled bad. And his carburetor got loose and bent out somehow. Nothing I can't set right."

"What do you need me for?"

"The engine's sitting deep in a narrow bay. It'll be a whole lot easier if you hand me the tools when I need 'em." He rowed a few strokes in silence. Then he said,

"You went out last night after I told you not to, didn't you?"

Shad shifted uncomfortably. "Got you a job," he said.

"Guess you did." Mr. Faherty eased up on the oars and let the boat drift. He glanced shyly at his son. "You know, you have to stop interfering. I don't want to see you hurt."

Shad, sensing what his father was about to say, tried not to listen. He let his fingers dangle in the water. They made little whirlpools. Deeper, dark minnows darted.

"It's hard around here," his father said. "Wasn't always. But it is now. There's nothing to be done about it. So we don't need to make more trouble than we've got, do we?"

Shad kept his eyes on the water.

"Your going out last night—the second time—wasn't the end of the world. Even worked out. I'll give you that. But look here, Shad, I've got to be able to trust you. I'd told you not to go out. Do you understand me?" His voice lowered. "I'm speaking man to man. You and me. I need you to understand."

"Yes, sir."

"Look at me. Let me see your eyes."

Shad glanced up.

"When I tell you to do something, I expect you to do it. And you have to be square with me. Sure, I got upset last night with that business with Kinlow. But you're the last one I want to fight. So, I need your word. You're old enough to give me that." He leaned forward. "I need

· · · 71

your word that you won't do anything like that again. Can I have it?" He gazed into Shad's face, looking for an answer. He seemed to be begging.

His father's expression reminded Shad of the night before, when he came back from speaking to Kinlow. He had looked so beaten. Again, it made Shad feel pain. "Don't you want to get rid of Kinlow?" he whispered.

As though stung, Mr. Faherty drew back. "I'm not just talking about him."

"He's beat you out, hasn't he?"

"Lots of things have beat me out. He's only one of them."

Shad wondered what his father would do if Brian did tell about his going into Kinlow's house. "What do you want to happen?" he asked.

"I gave up wanting a long time ago."

"Why?"

Mr. Faherty just shook his head. He didn't seem to have an answer.

"Is that all we can do, give up?" Shad demanded.

Mr. Faherty shook his head again. "Come on, boy," he urged. "We need you, and your word, and your help. You can give it."

Shad knew what he had to say. "Yes, sir," he lied. "You have it."

"Good enough," said his father with obvious relief. His face cleared. Dropping the oars into the water, he used a few sweeping strokes to bring them alongside *The Vole.*

Shad didn't even want to look at him.

* * *

The Vole was as fancy a boat as Shad had thought it
would be. Neat, even pretty—everything was first-rate.
The fittings were shiny, the wood glossy. It was a rich
man's boat such as Shad had never been on before.

On the aft deck Mr. Faherty had the hatches up, revealing the engine well. His tools were spread out on the
deck on a piece of oilcloth so the deck wouldn't get dirty.

Mr. Faherty let himself down into the well and began
to work. As he called for the tools he needed, Shad
handed them down.

"Where's Mr. Nevill?" Shad asked after a while.

"I took him ashore. Said he wanted to see the island."

"What do you think of him?"

"Rich as cream. And just as smooth. He doesn't know
the first thing about boats, I'll tell you that. I wouldn't be
surprised if he did the damage to the motor himself."

"What do you mean?" asked Shad, instantly alert.

"This here is a funny way for things to go wrong,"
said Mr. Faherty, tapping the boat's motor. "If you ask
me, something did go wrong, nothing important. Only
he must have tried to fix it himself. See, the coupling here
has been yanked off. Forced back on. Couldn't have been
more stupid if he'd *meant* to bust it."

"On purpose?" asked Shad.

"Well, no, I don't suppose. But I'll bet a dollar bill he
did the worst part. Not that he'd admit it."

"Does he have a radio?" Shad asked.

"Lord, yes," his father replied. "Twice as much and
twice as powerful as anyone'll ever need. Regular power

· · · 73

station. Some smart salesman must have sold him a bill of goods about a mile long. Took him for what he's worth. But then, I suppose he's worth a lot. Wonder how he makes his money."

"He told me," said Shad. "Insurance."

"Something," said his father.

As his father worked, Shad watched silently. He was wondering exactly who Mr. Nevill was, what his connection with Kinlow was, why he had come just then. He thought of the circled Monday on Kinlow's calendar. Next Monday. He wondered what was going to happen then, if it was as important as it looked. If he knew the answer to that, maybe he'd have answers to his other questions. Maybe he'd know enough to put them all in jail for a million years, a million, jillion miles away.

A voice from across the bay broke into his thoughts. It was Mr. Nevill calling from the dock. He wanted to get back to his boat.

Mr. Faherty sent Shad.

Mr. Nevill clambered down the dock ladder into the skiff, and Shad immediately began to pull back to *The Vole.*

"I really appreciate your telling me about your dad," said Nevill. He was sitting in the stern seat, his legs thrust forward. "He's promised to fix things up as quickly as possible."

Shad rowed in silence, feeling that Mr. Nevill was just making phony talk.

"A nice place, here," said Mr. Nevill. "What I like most about traveling is that I get to see new places, meet people I wouldn't ordinarily run into. Do you travel much?"

"No, sir."

"You go to the mainland, though, I bet, every chance you get."

"Well . . . yes."

After a moment Mr. Nevill remarked, "Things are pretty hard around here, aren't they?"

"Yes, sir," said Shad, feeling uncomfortable under Mr. Nevill's scrutiny.

"You don't have to row so fast, do you? Let's just sit and enjoy the view."

Reluctantly, Shad lifted the oars.

"Nice to live here, I should think," said Mr. Nevill. "Do you like it?"

"Yes, sir."

"Go to school here?"

"Don't have a school."

"No one to teach you reading and writing?"

"My ma."

"I see," said Nevill. "Awful lot of empty houses," he went on to say after a moment. "What happened to the people?"

"Gone off."

"Looking for work, I suppose," Nevill said. "I did see one house that looked all right, though. Even had a new fence around it. Up near the north end. Do you know the one I mean?"

Shad stared up at Mr. Nevill, trying to figure out what he was after. Obviously he was asking about Kinlow's house. The thought suddenly came to him that perhaps Mr. Nevill had seen him there, had seen him spying.

"Do you know the one I mean?" repeated Mr. Nevill.

"No, sir," said Shad softly.

"You must," insisted Nevill. "I found it when I was out walking. I got thirsty, and thought I'd get some water. Looked like the only house with people living in it. For a moment I thought I saw you. Did I?"

Shad felt dry in the throat. "No, sir," he said.

"Well, anyway, who does live there?"

Shad avoided Nevill's eyes. "Not sure where you mean."

"I'd have thought you'd know everything about this island. You keep your eyes open, don't you? You like to know what's going on."

Shad wasn't sure, but he thought there was a bit of smile in Mr. Nevill's look.

"I mind my own business," Shad got out. To cover his confusion, he began to row again as hard as he could.

"Tell you what," said Nevill, his eyes still fixed on Shad. "When the repairs are all done, how about coming to the mainland with me? Just for larks. Ice-cream soda. Moving-picture show. It'll be my way of saying thanks for the tip. What do you say?"

Shad, afraid to say anything lest Mr. Nevill drag something out of him, just rowed.

For the rest of the way, Nevill said nothing. But he kept looking curiously at Shad. Shad wished he knew what Nevill was thinking.

On the boat, Mr. Nevill stood by the engine well and looked down. "How's it coming?" he asked.

"Fine, just fine," said Mr. Faherty, bending over the motor.

"How long do you think it'll take?"

"Be ready tonight."

"Tonight!" Nevill seemed truly surprised.

"Yes, sir."

"I wasn't expecting anything that fast. I thought I'd be here a week at least."

"No, nothing like that." Mr. Faherty looked up out of the well. "You have somebody work on this before?"

"No, why?"

"It's like someone put things together every which way but right."

"Could have been me," confessed Nevill, turning slightly red. "I thought I'd have a go at it myself. Made things worse, did I?"

"Don't you worry. I'll have it right soon enough."

"Don't hurry on my account," said Nevill. "I rather like it here. I've a mind to stay awhile. It's so quiet and peaceful. Think anyone would object if I stayed out the week?"

"Don't know why they should."

"At least till next Monday. And, say," said Nevill, "I

· · · 77

thought I might take your boy here over to the mainland one of these days. I want to show my appreciation."

"No need."

"I'd like to. It'll be some time before I leave. Sunday, maybe. Monday at the latest." He turned to Shad. "That a deal?"

The word "Monday" reverberated in Shad's head. Monday, when something was going to happen. It was obvious to Shad that it was Monday that Nevill wanted him off the island. Though he murmured a "Yes, sir," he knew there was no way he would leave the island. He would not go with Nevill.

···10

MR. NEVILL ROWED SHAD AND HIS FATHER BACK to the dock at a little before seven o'clock. The repairs had been completed. Mr. Nevill had even given Mr. Faherty two dollars extra for getting the work done so fast. When Shad thought of the money he had already paid, it seemed a lot. But because the money was tied to Kinlow, Shad wished they didn't need it.

As they walked across to the house, Shad's father was in a good mood, with only good things to say about Mr. Nevill. He reminded Shad about the offer to take him to the mainland. "That's more than generous," said Mr. Faherty. "That's grand."

"I don't want to go," Shad announced.

His father merely looked at his own hands. They were, as always, dirty with grease. Then, turning to Shad, he said, "You don't know a good thing when you have it."

When they walked into the house, Shad took one look at his mother and knew something was wrong. She said nothing, but her mouth was tight. She didn't even greet Mr. Faherty, or ask him about the job. When he gave her the rest of Nevill's money, she silently put it away.

"Where's Brian?" asked Shad, beginning to get an understanding of what had happened.

"Back room," his mother said.

Shad went to the door of their room, opened it, and looked in. Brian was lying on the bed. He turned over. The two boys looked at each other. Their eyes had only to meet for Shad to know that his brother had told his mother what he had overheard. Quickly, Shad turned back into the main room. His mother was whispering to his father. When she drew away, his father said, "Tell Brian to come out here."

Shad beckoned and Brian came edging out of the room, avoiding looking at Shad. Mr. Faherty sat down at the table. So did Mrs. Faherty. She told Brian to come over and sit next to her.

"Shad," she said, "you sit too."

Shad, his heart beating hard, sat down.

Then Mrs. Faherty put a hand on Brian's shoulder.

"Now," she said, "tell your father what you told me this afternoon. Shad, you pay attention."

Shad, expecting the worst, glared at his brother with hatred. Brian still wouldn't look at him.

"Go on, say it," urged his mother. "If it's true you've got nothing to worry about."

Brian, as if asking for something, stole a nervous glance at Shad.

"What is it?" demanded Mr. Faherty, his voice edgy.

"Go on," Mrs. Faherty said to Brian again.

"I heard him talking," began Brian. His voice was small. "To Davey."

"You didn't hear," Shad cut in. "You came *spying* at our place. *Last night,* too."

"Let him talk," said Mrs. Faherty.

Brian took a breath, then spoke to his mother all in a rush, without once looking at Shad or his father. "He and Davey were saying how they were going to catch Mr. Kinlow and put him in jail. Shad was saying it last night and he was saying it this afternoon. I heard him."

"See," cut in Shad. "He went out last night. He admits it."

Mrs. Faherty, however, was looking at her husband. Then she turned to Shad.

"Is that true, what he said?" asked Shad's father after a moment. His hands, on the table, were tightly clasped.

"He was sneaking around," said Shad. "Listening when he had no right to."

Mr. Faherty shook his head. "Is that true, what he

said?" he asked Shad again. "You and Davey planning to do something to Kinlow?"

"You hate him too," said Shad.

"I asked you something."

"He makes you do whatever he wants you to. He makes everybody. As if he were king or something."

Mr. Faherty opened and shut his hands nervously. Then he rubbed his face with them, squeezed his mouth.

Shad turned to his mother. "I've got a way to get him. I'll get him away from here for *good.*"

"I thought," said Mr. Faherty, "you agreed to have nothing to do with him."

"*I* didn't say that," Shad threw back.

"For your own good, Shad—" began Mrs. Faherty.

"*His* good, is what you mean," Shad cut in. "Next Monday—"

"Stop it!" cried his father, banging his hand hard on the table.

Shad jumped. Brian began to sniffle. Mrs. Faherty got up, pushing her chair away, and leaned against the window frame, staring out, her arms crossed over her middle.

"It's a free country," Shad mumbled.

"It isn't!" cried his father. "That man does what he wants because he's powerful. There is *nothing* we can do about it. Do you want to get yourself killed? Your brother? Your mother? Me? Do you think he wouldn't?"

"Look what he's done to you. . . ." tried Shad.

Mr. Faherty shook his head. "You don't know what you're talking about."

"Mr. Nevill—" Shad started to say.

"Mr. Nevill has nothing to do with anything here!"

"That's how much *you* know!" Shad threw back. "He came to Kinlow's house when I was in there—" Too late, Shad realized what he had said.

Complete silence. They were all staring at him.

"In his house?" his mother echoed. *"In* it?"

Shad struggled to hold back tears. "He was off the island," he said. "There wasn't any way he—"

"You damn fool kid," Mr. Faherty said between his teeth. "You stupid, stupid fool. You don't listen to *anything* you're told, do you?"

Shad hung his head.

"You're going to stay in this house, you hear?" said his father. *"Here.* From now on you're not going *anywhere,* unless you get permission. *Nowhere!"*

"But—"

"Or," said his father, not pausing, "by the good Lord, I'll—" He stopped in mid-sentence. Shad could see that his father had remembered his previous threat, the whipping.

Neither spoke. They only looked at each other.

"Go on," said Mr. Faherty, his eyes shifting away, his voice trembling. "Get into your room. I'm going to make you understand that what I tell you is what I mean. Go . . . on."

Suddenly frightened, Shad appealed silently to his mother. Her face was white, her mouth clenched shut. He looked at Brian. There were tears running down his cheeks. He looked at his father. His father's face was pale. Shad could see the twitch of straining muscles along his jaw.

Shad got up, knocking his chair over behind him. Clumsily, he picked it up, set it right. Then he turned to his father in mute supplication.

"Go on," his father said again.

Slowly, Shad retreated into the back room.

Shad had never been whipped before. The belt had only hung in the room, an unused threat. There had been warnings, but nothing more. The other times, his father had backed off, or found reasons for not going through with it. This time, Shad knew, it would be different.

Shad looked at the window and thought about running away. He could have. He wanted to. But he didn't.

He waited, listening.

No sounds came from the front room. Shad began to wonder if his father would come at all.

Footsteps approached the door. They hesitated. Shad knew then that his father was afraid, just as he was afraid. He turned his back to the door, not wanting his father to see what he was feeling.

The door opened. Shad could feel his father standing there, trying to find the strength to come in. Shad felt the sweat on his own body.

Mr. Faherty walked in. He shut the door behind him.

Shad forced himself to turn around. They faced each other. On his father's face there was a sick look, the same as when he had come back after Kinlow had threatened him. He looked old. Exhausted. One hand was bunched into a fist. The other hand, open, kept rubbing against his side as if the side hurt. He kept swallowing.

"I warned you, didn't I?" Mr. Faherty's voice was as dry as sand.

"Yes, sir."

"And I told you what would happen, didn't I?"

"Yes, sir."

"You don't give me any choice, do you?"

"No, sir."

"Is that what you want? You testing me?"

Shad said nothing.

His father looked away. Then he said, "Get the belt."

Shad moved across the room, took the belt from the nail in the wall, came back and handed it over. Mr. Faherty took it, studied it as it lay across his still-dirty fingers. Shad backed off to the opposite side of the room, as far away from his father as he could get.

"It's for you," his father said. "Your own good. You don't listen to me. You never do. You're putting all of us in a bad way. I'm not backing down this time." The belt, dangling from his hand, just touched the floor. "I'm the one that takes care of you. Me and your mother. We're in charge."

"Prove it," said Shad, only to be instantly sorry he had spoken.

Mr. Faherty's face turned red. "Turn around," he said, speaking just above a whisper.

Shad stood motionless, telling himself that he would

not turn. He never would. He hated his father. Hated his mother. Hated his brother. Hated everything. There was nothing they could make him do. *Nothing.*

He stood there, defiant, looking at his father.

"Turn around," his father said again, his face showing his grief.

Seeing how hard it was for his father, Shad felt himself pierced with pain. He suddenly wanted to tell his father that he wouldn't do anything bad anymore, that he would promise to keep away from Kinlow, and that he would mean it.

Only he couldn't get himself to say it. Couldn't get his mouth to form the words. All he heard himself saying was, "It's Kinlow's fault. He's the one you should be whipping, not me. I hate him. And you hate him too."

"Drop your overalls."

Shad didn't move.

"Go on. Drop 'em."

Mechanically, Shad worked the buttons on the straps, pulling the straps down.

"Pull them down. All the way." His father's voice was shaking.

Shad got the overalls past his drawers, then stuffed them down around his ankles. He shivered.

"You have to obey me," his father said, as though to convince himself.

Shad closed his eyes.

"Turn around," his father said.

This time Shad did turn. He pressed his arms to his

sides, shut his teeth so tightly his jaw ached. He swore he wouldn't cry, wouldn't flinch or jump, wouldn't do anything, not a thing. He just waited to be hit, waited for it to happen.

Only nothing did.

Shad opened his eyes, and slowly turned around.

His father was standing there, shoulders bent, head down. He was holding the belt in his hands, staring at it, twisting it. Then he dropped the belt to the floor and covered his face with his hands.

"I don't want to hurt you," he finally said. The words were faint.

Shad remained motionless.

"There's too much anger," his father said with effort. He pulled his hands from his face. He was crying. "A body tries to stand up in front of that anger," he said, "tries to stand between it and the ones . . . he cares for." He swung away from Shad, as if he had said something shameful. "I can't hurt you," he said slowly. "Pull up your things."

Shad pulled up his overalls, fumbling as he buttoned the straps. Then he stood there, wishing there was something he could say.

For a moment neither spoke.

It was Shad who broke the silence. "I know where Kinlow keeps that liquor," he said.

His father shook his head. "I don't want to know."

"I'm going to get Kinlow."

Mr. Faherty said nothing.

"I'm going to tell Mr. Sheraton—that government man, the one who checks that gauge. He's going to help me get rid of Kinlow."

"No one's going to help you."

"I'll get a reward for helping. He said so."

"You won't."

"I will. And I'll give it to you, and Ma. All of it. I don't want it."

"Why?" asked his father. "Why are you doing all this?"

"Because . . ." said Shad, trying to find the words, the reasons. "'Cause of what he did . . . to you . . . to Ma."

Startled, Mr. Faherty gazed up at Shad. "Because of that?" he said. The paleness of his face gave way to a deep flush of shame.

"Yes, sir."

"Then I'm sorry for you," he whispered. "And me. And all of us. Sorry for the whole world. You're always saying, 'It's a free country.' But nothing is free, nothing."

When he realized that his father wasn't going to say any more, Shad took a step forward. His father didn't move. Shad walked past him, out of the room. He went past his mother, his brother, out of the house.

No one stopped him.

11

SHAD WENT WALKING. NO PLACE IN PARTICULAR, only walking, away from any place he might be seen. He didn't want to see anyone, either. He wanted to be alone, tucked into himself.

If anything, he felt more frightened than he had before. He had won out over his father. But the more he thought about it, the clearer it became that he hadn't really wanted to. If his father was so helpless, if his parents couldn't do anything, either of them, not even to him, their son, how could he, Shad, think of doing something to Kinlow? And if it was true that there was nothing to do except what Kinlow told them to do . . . like slaves . . .

The bitterness Shad felt ran deep.

It was dark when he got home. Lit by the kerosene lamp, the house seemed tired, worn out, shabby, and small.

His father wasn't there. Coming home, Shad had recognized him on the dock, sitting with some of the other men. Their cigarettes had glowed faintly, had moved like fireflies trapped in a bottle.

In the main room of their house his mother was by the table, sewing. When Shad came in she looked up from her work. "Where've you been?" she asked quietly.

"Walking."

"I was worried."

Shad shrugged.

"You want your dinner?"

"I guess."

He sat at the table. Mrs. Faherty brought him a plate of fish and potato. Then she went back to her sewing.

Shad, not feeling at all hungry, poked at his food with his fork. "I didn't mean to make him cry," he said at last.

She lifted her head to study Shad for a moment, then bowed over her work again. "Wasn't you," she said.

"What was it, then?"

"He's scared."

"About what?"

"Everything."

Shad had no stomach for food. He put down his fork. "What should I do?" he asked.

His mother shook her head. "Don't ask me. You're going to do it your way anyway, aren't you? You won."

Shad felt numb. "I didn't mean to win."

"You're trying to get to next year by crossing a bridge."

"What do you mean?"

"Going out of your way to get something, when you'd do better standing still. Maybe it'll come, maybe it won't. Has nothing to do with you."

"Ma . . . do you want me to be scared?"

She lifted her eyes from her work. "There's no shame in giving up. Most folks do. No shame at all."

Shad waited for her to say more, but there was only the soft flutter of her hands, sewing. He got up, left his plate by the sink, then went into the back room and closed the door.

Brian was asleep.

Shad looked at him in the faint light. He remembered that he should be angry with him. But he wasn't; he didn't have the energy for it. He just got undressed and crawled into bed.

Over and over he thought about what had happened. All he knew was that he had to do something, something to show his mother and father that it wasn't so hopeless. If he could get Kinlow, it would make things so different. It would be like giving something to his parents. It would make them understand why he stood up to them the way he had.

But what could he do?

There was one thing: he could get to Mr. Sheraton and start telling him what he knew. He could leave a message for him in the rain-gauge box.

But how, he wondered, could he even write a message, a letter? The truth was, he had never written one before. But that was the way to do it. Somehow he would do it. He would. And knowing that, he fell asleep.

Next morning when Shad woke, he was alone in the bed. In the front room he heard voices. Though he didn't want to talk with his parents, or Brian, he felt he needed to talk to someone. Maybe Davey had changed his mind. Besides, he knew he ought to tell Davey that Brian had told. Davey might get in trouble too.

Shad dressed quickly and silently, slid open the window, and went to find Davey.

Davey was surprised and uneasy to see Shad. He didn't want to go to their house. Instead they walked along the beach, moving northward away from the dock.

"What happened?" Davey demanded.

"Brian told my folks," Shad said.

Davey stopped short. "He say anything about me?" he asked.

"Sure."

Davey looked ill.

"You might as well help now," said Shad. "You're in it anyway."

"What are you going to do?"

"I've got some evidence, haven't I?" said Shad. "And when Monday comes, I bet I have a whole lot more."

"What's happening Monday?"

"I'm not sure. Something, something important. And when I learn everything, I'll tell that government man, Mr. Sheraton."

Davey thought about it all. "I can't!" he finally blurted out. "Honest. I'd be no good at it. Anyway, you don't really want me. I'd be too scared."

"Everybody's scared," said Shad.

"You're not."

"Is that what you think?" asked Shad, surprised.

"It's the way you're acting."

Shad studied his friend. Then, with a feeling that it was of no use to argue, he walked away. Once, in spite of himself, he glanced back. Davey was standing where he had left him, looking miserable. Shad tried to tell himself he didn't care.

He headed back home.

When he got there, his father was busy in his back workroom. Brian was at the table with his mother, practicing his letters. They looked up at Shad when he came in, but no one said anything.

Shad went into the bedroom in search of a piece of paper. All he could find was a blank page at the end of his own reading book. He tore it out.

Shad didn't write well. He knew he could talk a lot better. Still, he couldn't just sit by the box and wait for

the man. People might get suspicious. Writing was the
best way. He wrote:

Mr. Sheradan

There are smuglers working the island

I know them and I know where they put
the lickor.

Thats not all.

I can show you how to cetch ther boss
on monday.

You have to give me a sine. Ill watch.

And I have to talk to you.

For a long while Shad debated whether or not to put his
name to the bottom of the letter. In the end, he decided
not to.

Folding the paper carefully, he went out and headed
straight for the southern point.

It was warm that day, almost humid—a taste of the coming summer. Soft, easy air floated in from the sea. Gulls
swooped and turned their backs to the sun, gray-white
wings shaping the air the way Shad thought angels' wings
might do.

He climbed to the top of a dune and stood staring out
over his island. It was so empty, peaceful and quiet. It
made him feel strange to know how much else there was.

Was he the only one who knew? And if other people knew, why didn't *they* do something? It was so strange to think that he was the only one willing to help the people on the island. All the others, he guessed, were too scared for themselves. But he was scared too, so scared that if he didn't do something, or at least try, he'd be like his father and mother the night before. If he didn't take a chance, he'd be like them.

Like a slave . . .

He folded and unfolded his letter, creasing it until it was as soft as an old dollar bill. Then—on impulse—he held the letter high over his head, as high as he could reach. A lightning rod, he thought. And he shouted, "I'm going to do it!" In his mind he dared anyone, anything to snatch the letter from him, to strike him down to smithereens.

But only the gulls wheeled and whipped through the warm, wet air.

Hauling down his letter, Shad went toward the point.

When he made out Sheraton's box, he slowed his pace, patting his pocket where he'd tucked the letter. Then he made himself take a hard look around to make certain no one was near.

No one was.

Mindful, though, of how Sheraton had been able to hide from him, Shad didn't go directly to the box. Rather, he circled it, keeping his distance. Even though the place seemed deserted, he sat down and told himself to wait patiently.

Not that he was expecting anyone. If anything, he was near praying that no one would come.

After about twenty minutes, when he had seen no one, he felt certain that he wasn't being watched. Moving slowly, he went to the box and tugged the door open, then he placed his letter beside the cup. Sheraton would see it instantly. Quickly, Shad closed the box door. It snapped shut with a click. For a moment Shad stood there. Then he turned and ran.

···12

THE NEXT TWO DAYS WERE DIFFICULT. THEY seemed to last forever. Shad quickly grew tired of waiting for things to happen. He wished he knew exactly when Sheraton might come and give him some answer, some sign.

For much of the first day Shad spent his time watching *The Vole* and Kinlow's house. Kinlow had not returned either. Shad almost wished he'd come back. At least he could watch him. As for Nevill, he didn't seem to do much of anything. He chatted with the men on the dock.

He fished. That was all. As far as Shad knew, he didn't venture close to Kinlow's house again.

On the second day, Thursday, it rained in the morning. Shad played "Go Fish" with Brian for what felt like a thousand times.

Once, when they were in the middle of a game, Brian said, "Shad."

"What?"

"I'm sorry I told."

"Doesn't matter," returned Shad, not wanting to discuss things with Brian.

Brian didn't talk about it again.

That afternoon, after it cleared, Davey came over and asked if Shad wanted to come out. Shad agreed, still hoping his friend might change his mind about helping.

They went out, and, as they often did, they searched some of the empty houses. That was the way they had found the crackers and the tin of sardines. Their rule was that anything they found when looking would go to their place.

In one abandoned house they found a good pencil, its eraser intact. In another, in a back room, against a doorframe, Shad noticed markings that told how tall a kid was at different times. The markings stopped at about Shad's height. Shad wondered how tall that kid was now.

Shad and Davey had a decent time. But Davey didn't say anything about the Kinlow business, and Shad was determined not to bring it up. A couple of times he thought Davey was going to talk about it, but he never did.

Friday was another boring day. Nevill hiked about the island, while Shad, at a safe distance, tracked him. He didn't learn anything.

At home everything was very quiet. No one spoke much. Shad kept feeling that they were waiting to see what—if anything—he would do.

Saturday was one of the days that Sheraton usually checked his rain gauge. That morning, Shad, restless and impatient, made up his mind to go where he could at least watch and see if Sheraton got the letter. He promised himself that he wouldn't do anything more than watch.

He set out early, long before he needed to, on the small cross-island pathway he had taken to the marsh ferry on Monday.

Shad came to the place that gave the best view of Kinlow's house, the place he had watched from earlier in the week. As he gazed at the house, the first thing he noticed was that the green streamer was atop the flagpole. Then he saw that Kinlow and his two men were sitting around the front yard table. They had come back a day earlier than usual.

Shad suddenly understood what the green flag meant: it was Kinlow's way of saying—to someone—that he was there. But who was the message for? Nevill? Yes, probably Nevill.

He watched Kinlow's house for almost an hour, but when nothing at all happened, he went on.

As he drew close to the ferry landing, Shad saw Mr. Jefferson pedaling at his wheel, drawing close. To Shad's great relief, Sheraton was aboard.

Shad, lying atop the dune that overlooked the ferry landing, ducked behind the crest, remembering his promise to himself not to let Sheraton see him. When he looked up again, Sheraton, knapsack on his back, was already marching along the shore. Mr. Jefferson, without an immediate return fare, had set himself up against a boulder and was just waiting.

When Sheraton had ambled off a good way down the beach, Shad stood up. Mr. Jefferson spotted him right away.

"Shad!" he called.

Shad looked around.

"People know what you're doing!" cried Mr. Jefferson.

Startled, Shad just stared at the old man; then, feeling a greater sense of urgency than ever, he followed after Sheraton, staying behind the dune.

As Sheraton had done before, he moved along easily, stopping now and again to gather shells. Still, it wasn't long before he reached his box.

Shad watched from a distance.

Casually, Mr. Sheraton set his knapsack down and took out his binoculars. He scanned the bay for a long time. Only then did he turn to the box and open the door.

He paused, then turned and looked over his shoulder, as if to see whether anyone was watching. Then he reached inside the box. Shad saw him pull out the letter, and for a moment simply hold it in his hand. Then, carefully, Sheraton unfolded it, and took a long time to read it.

With care, he started to put the paper into his jacket pocket, only to unfold it and read it once more.

Then, apparently satisfied, he put it away and took his measurements. When that was done, he closed the box, pulled on his knapsack, and began to walk slowly back along the shore toward the ferry. His face was a study in concentration.

When Mr. Sheraton passed right below where Shad was hiding, Shad couldn't hold himself back. It was impossible to wait anymore. Besides, he quickly told himself, if Mr. Sheraton left, how would he know about the coming Monday, which seemed so important?

Shad stood up. "Hey!" he called.

Sheraton stopped instantly, turning to try to find where the voice had come from, shielding his eyes from the sun with his hand. When he spotted Shad, the two stared at each other across the fifty feet that separated them. Then Sheraton began to take long strides up the sloping dune. Ten feet from Shad he stopped.

"You hid yourself better this time," he said, flipping the hair out of his eyes. "I got your message."

"Can we catch them?" Shad asked right away.

Sheraton cocked his head slightly to one side, then again tossed the hair out of his eyes. "Maybe," he said. "What did you want to tell me?"

Going no closer, Shad began to speak. He told Sheraton most of what he knew about Kinlow—how Kinlow first came, and when. What he did. How he frightened people, beat them up, chased them off the island. Shad explained how the smuggling was done, the names of people he knew who were involved. He even told Sheraton about Mr. Nevill.

When he finished, Shad thought Sheraton was impressed. "You know everything, don't you?" he said. He wasn't smiling.

"I can take you to Kinlow's house," said Shad, who had been saving the best for last. "That's where he keeps the liquor."

"How can you be so sure?"

"I saw it."

"Through a window?"

"I went in."

This time Sheraton showed real surprise. *"Inside the house?"*

"Yes, sir."

Sheraton shook his head. "You're quite the Old Sleuth."

"Yes, sir," said Shad, feeling pleased.

Sheraton said, "Those other people you spoke about, the ones who work with Kinlow, aren't they friends, neighbors?"

"They're only doing it because they're scared of what'll happen to them if they quit," said Shad.

"Not for the money?"

"I don't think so. Not now. Kinlow used to give them more. Gives them hardly anything now. He's a thief both ways."

"You know what'll happen to your friends if Kinlow gets caught, don't you?"

"No, sir."

"They'll be taken too."

"He's the crook."

"You better think about that some more," said Sheraton. Then he went on, "This Mr. Nevill, tell me about him again."

Shad repeated what he knew.

"You're sure," said Sheraton, "that your father thinks he broke his engine himself?"

"Yes, sir."

"And, as far as you're concerned, that proves he's working with the smugglers?"

"I told you what I saw, what he did."

Sheraton became thoughtful. "What's the name of his boat?"

"*The Vole.*"

Sheraton took his notebook and pencil from his knapsack and wrote a few words. "From where?" he asked. "Did you notice?"

"Greenport, New York."

"You've got a good memory."

"Yes, sir. Can we catch Kinlow on Monday?"

"You're in a big hurry."

"I hate him."

"Why?"

For a moment Shad thought about his father, and then his mother's words: "No shame in giving up."

"You going to tell me why you hate him?" asked Sheraton.

"Because he scares people," said Shad.

"Look here," said Sheraton. "This Nevill, he's the one who puzzles me. Who do you think he is?"

"I don't know. Maybe he's Kinlow's boss."

"You're just guessing. It's the same as I told you before—I need evidence. But you leave that to me, do you understand? I'll find out who he is."

"And I'll watch too," said Shad. "You do work for the government, don't you?"

"How many people know all these things you've been telling me?" asked Sheraton, ignoring Shad's question.

"I don't know. Maybe they all do. Or most of it. But they're scared."

"Aren't you?" demanded Sheraton, looking curiously at Shad.

"I don't want to be. Can we get him Monday?" Shad asked again. "Something big's going to happen Monday. I just know it."

Sheraton was silent. Then he said, "You're going to have to promise not to tell a soul about any of this till I give you permission. Can you give me your promise?"

"Yes, sir. Cross my heart."

"Monday . . ." he said, as much to himself as to Shad. "What time?"

"I could meet you at the ferry," said Shad. "By ten at night, or close to it. They'll have stored their liquor in Kinlow's house by then."

"I might be able to be there."

"See, that way," said Shad, "you wouldn't have to arrest anyone but Kinlow and his two men."

"You've thought it all out, haven't you?"

"I tried."

Sheraton appeared to make up his mind. "Well, Shad," he said, "I can't promise anything. I might not even be able to come. And if I don't . . ."

"You'll try, won't you?" Shad begged.

Sheraton looked at Shad searchingly. "Yes, I'll try," he said. Then, abruptly, he turned and began to walk along the water's edge, heading for the ferry.

Shad watched him go. Somehow, he felt disappointed. It was as if he had expected that just speaking to Sheraton would make things better. But as he watched Sheraton move along the beach, he understood that nothing was settled yet. He'd have to wait until Monday.

13

THE NEXT DAY, SUNDAY, SHAD TRIED TO KEEP OUT of trouble by doing only what he was supposed to do. He wanted no one to be suspicious of him. A couple of times he thought of telling his mother and father what he had done—about Mr. Sheraton—and that things were going to get better. But he decided against it, sure they wouldn't approve. As it was, from time to time his parents looked at him as if they were about to ask questions. But they didn't. Brian, too, just watched and kept his distance.

Once, Shad went down to the dock where the men sat,

thinking he might hear them say something important about Monday. But as he drew near, they stopped talking. He could feel them watching him. Bennett was there. As Shad went by, the old man roared out, "Remember!"

Shad jumped, and, embarrassed, went out to the end of the dock and sat there alone.

His one big worry was that Mr. Nevill would come by and try to make him go along with him to the mainland, as he had said he would. But Sunday passed without *The Vole*'s even being seen in the bay. It was almost dark before it returned.

Shad wondered where Nevill had gone.

Monday was gray. The sea was up, with tides running high. Shad and Brian spent the morning doing the lessons Mrs. Faherty had set for them. She did mending. Mr. Faherty was there too, working on some broken tools. Shad could tell he was nervous from the way he worked. Usually, he was slow and patient. That morning, he wasn't.

At about eleven there was a knock on the door. It made them all jump.

Brian ran to open the door. Mr. Nevill was there, smiling, dressed in his whites, cap in hand.

"Good morning," he said, stepping in without waiting for an invitation.

"Morning," said Mr. Faherty, awkwardly coming to his feet.

Shad, heart racing, looked on.

"I'd promised to take Shad to the mainland," said Mr. Nevill. "Today's the day. I should be heading home before dark. I thought, this being my last day, and if you had no objections, I still had time for one last run to the mainland. We'd have to go right now, though. . . . My treat."

"That's very kind of you," said Mrs. Faherty.

"Not at all," said Nevill. "I'm sorry to be leaving your island. I've had a pleasant time. It's a lovely place. And everyone's been most hospitable. I intend to come again. . . . Well, skipper," he said to Shad, "how about it?"

Shad didn't know what to say. He was certain that Nevill was only trying to get him out of the way, and would never get him back by evening. He wasn't going to go. He just stood there silently.

His father and mother were looking at him.

"Shad?" his mother prompted.

"I'll go if Shad doesn't want to," put in Brian.

Shad looked over to Brian and realized that Brian had no idea who Mr. Nevill really was.

"Some other time," said Mr. Nevill with a good-natured laugh. "It's your brother I want to take now. How about it, sport? Maybe we can find a picture show. How about Laurel and Hardy? Like them? Then we'll find something to eat. Get you home before it's too late."

"It's very decent of you," said Mr. Faherty.

"Well?" asked Nevill once more. He was smiling broadly.

Shad, aware that they were all looking at him, waiting for him to say something, was still trying desperately to think of how to get out of it.

After a moment, Nevill said, "I'll wait outside. You can make up your mind and let me know." He stepped out, shutting the door behind him.

"I'm not going," Shad announced the moment Mr. Nevill was gone.

"Why?" demanded his father.

"I'm not," repeated Shad.

"That's not an answer."

"I don't want to."

His mother came over to him, pushed back his hair, straightened his shirt. "He's doing you a nice favor," she said. "You don't get to go to the mainland that often."

"I can go with you tomorrow," said Shad.

"Maybe not," she retorted.

Mr. Faherty opened the front door. "He'll be right out," he called.

Still trying to find a way to escape, Shad got up slowly and moved outside, hardly looking at the waiting Nevill.

"Are you sure, now?" Nevill asked him.

Mrs. Faherty had followed Shad out. "He's just shy," she said.

"We'll have a swell time," said Nevill. And he began to walk toward the dock, where he had left his skiff.

Shad, head down, but looking for his opportunity, followed a few paces behind. He knew his mother was watching from the door, probably his father too.

When Shad reached the middle of the street, he simply turned and began to run as fast as he could. His mother called after him. He kept running.

Only when he felt safe, unreachable, did Shad stop atop a dune and look back.

Mr. Nevill had returned to *The Vole*. Shad saw the water foam as the motor churned. Mr. Nevill hoisted his anchor. As he steered the boat around the channel bell and out of the bay, he turned in the direction that would take him to the mainland.

Shad stayed where he was. In that spot he would be able to see if anyone was coming after him.

Soon he concluded that no one was.

Shad knew that he would have to keep away from the dock area and any other place where his mother or father might be or might look for him. He wondered if they would look for him. The other night his mother had said he had won. Did that mean they would let him do whatever he wanted?

It crossed his mind that his running off the way he had might make Mr. Nevill suspicious. It might even cause him to change the plans for that night. But it was too late now to do anything about that.

Knowing he had to keep out of sight till dark, Shad wandered aimlessly over the island, restlessly moving from place to place. Then he decided he might as well go and watch Kinlow's house.

Nothing special seemed to be happening there at all. The worst was when one of the men came out and sat at the table, eating a sandwich. It made Shad realize he was terribly hungry.

In midafternoon they sent out a radio message. Shad wondered where the message was going, what it was about. Was it for Nevill? Would Nevill send a message back? Was it a message about him? He wondered, too, if Sheraton would come that night. What if Sheraton didn't show up? He couldn't bear the thought.

As the afternoon wore on, Shad grew hungrier. He thought about the food that he and Davey had hidden away in their house. He knew he could get to that. But their place was so close to the Front Street houses that he was afraid to go there in the daylight. He would have to wait until dark.

Shad started wandering again. For a while he waited near the ferry landing. The clouds were passing quickly, making the sky clear. The marsh seemed emptier than usual. The tide, extra high, had covered most of the salt-hay islands. Mr. Jefferson's boat was nowhere in view.

As the day turned to dusk, Shad could think of nothing but how hungry he was. He found himself edging closer to the bay side of the island. A quick check told him that *The Vole* hadn't returned. Shad wondered if he would ever see it, or Mr. Nevill, again.

Finally, though it was still only dusk, Shad decided he could safely go to the empty house and get the food.

He reached it easily enough, certain no one had noticed him. Quickly he slipped through the back door. Stepping over the broken floorboards, he made his way to the front room.

There, asleep on the floor, was Brian.

14

FOR A MOMENT SHAD JUST STOOD THERE, LOOKING at his brother, his anger rising. He strode over to Brian and shook his shoulder. Brian sat up and rubbed his eyes.

"What are you doing here?" demanded Shad. "Answer me!"

"I want to help."

"You can't."

"Why not?"

"You just can't, that's why not! Get out of here."

Brian didn't move.

"You don't even know what it's all about."

"I do too."

"What?"

"You're going to try and catch Mr. Kinlow. See, I know, don't I?"

"How'd you get here?"

Brian tried to smile. "Out the window. They don't know. They told me to go to bed early. Shad," said Brian, "I can help. I can. Anyway, I won't go back, and you can't make me."

Shad said nothing.

"I'll do what you tell me," tried Brian.

Shad wasn't sure what he should do or say, and he felt too hungry to think it through. He pulled out one of the cracker boxes and the sardine can from the storage place. After quickly devouring a few crackers, he opened the can with its key. He leaned back against a wall and ate greedily.

"Where'd you get the sardines?" asked Brian.

"Davey and I found them."

"He going to help you?"

"No."

"No one thinks you can catch Kinlow," said Brian. "I do."

Shad stopped eating, lifted his eyes, and looked at Brian through the growing darkness. "How come?"

"I just do."

"You're the only one," said Shad with disgust. He sucked his oily fingers clean.

"What do we do first?" Brian asked after a long pause.

"Look," said Shad, "I don't even know what I'm going to do. I mean, I know some. But not all. It could be really dangerous. You might get hurt."

"If I'm with you, I won't."

"How come you're so sure about me?"

"I just am."

Shad couldn't tell what he felt, irritation or pleasure. "You'd have to do everything I told you. No arguing."

"I know."

Shad finished off the crackers, then put the box and the empty sardine tin aside. From time to time he glanced at Brian. "Soon as it's really dark," he said finally, "I have to watch them come in with the boat. It's something special tonight. I don't know what, but I have to find out. Then I have to follow them, make sure it's all put in Kinlow's house. Can you do that with me?"

Brian nodded.

"See, that's the evidence I need. Then, at about ten, I have to get to the ferry landing. That Mr. Sheraton, I'm going to meet him there. You know him, don't you?"

Brian nodded again.

"He's a secret agent for the government," said Shad.

"How do you know?"

"He told me. And he'll bring other people with him, I bet. Then I'm going to take him to Kinlow's house. He'll arrest Kinlow and put him in jail."

"Shad?" said Brian after a moment.

"What?"

"Mr. Kinlow has a pistol."

"So what?"

"Nothing," said Brian. He looked across to his brother. "It sounds pretty easy."

"It will be. But you have to do what I tell you, and not mess things up."

"I won't."

After a moment Shad asked, "Have Ma or Dad been looking for me?"

"Ma wanted to. Dad said no. He said there was no use in looking if you didn't want to be found."

"He said that?"

"Yes. Shad?"

"What?"

"Ma was crying."

Shad said nothing.

"I don't like this place," said Brian with a sniff. "It stinks."

"Everything dead stinks," said Shad.

"Houses can't be dead."

"This one is."

"Shad?"

"What?"

"*Can* I go with you?"

"Maybe."

Brian understood that meant yes.

They waited.

Every so often Shad stood up, went to the front door, and looked at the sky, trying to calculate the time.

The moon had risen, but Shad knew it was still too early.

"Where'd you go before?" asked Brian.

"Just around."

"You watch Kinlow?"

"A bit. Just stay quiet now, will you?"

Brian said nothing for a while, then he said, "Do you think Kinlow guesses anything?"

"Stop bothering me!" cried Shad. "You said you'd do as I told you."

Brian clenched his mouth shut. But after five minutes he said, "There's almost a full moon tonight. We'll be able to see real good."

"Yeah."

"Will they see us too?"

"Doesn't matter," said Shad, but he hadn't thought of that.

In the end, Shad grew impatient. Though he knew it was still too early, he told Brian it was time to go.

"Now remember," he said. "You do what I tell you."

"I will."

They slipped out of the house and skirted back behind the row of Front Street houses, around to the north side of the dock. The moon, as Brian had said, was big and full. It was bright enough to make Shad decide it would be better to keep off the lower beach for a while. Hiding behind a clump of low bushes high on the beach, they waited.

"Look here," Shad suddenly whispered to Brian. "I'm glad you came. You're the only one who would. But if you want to change your mind, I'm not going to hold it against you. You can go if you want. But now's the time."

"I don't want to go," said Brian.

After about twenty more minutes had passed, someone walked to the far end of the dock and lit the lamp. When he walked back the snap of his heels beat hollow on the wooden planks. Shad couldn't recognize who it was.

"Need to get closer," he said.

Keeping low, Shad moved down the beach. Brian kept right behind him. They lay down. Shad kept his eyes on the dock. Brian gave him a nudge.

"What?"

"Look."

Shad looked in the direction Brian was pointing. From behind the Front Street houses, three men had appeared. For a moment they stayed in the shadows, but Shad was sure it was Kinlow and his two men.

One of the three moved down the street, along the wooden walkway. In moments Shad heard rapping. It was the warning.

As the boys watched, house lights began to go out. When their own house went dark, Brian nudged Shad again. Shad felt the way he had when he had gone far out to sea in an open boat, and the last bit of land had dropped from view. He wondered what his parents were thinking.

Soon, the row of twelve houses was completely dark. The houses looked dead.

Then, from far out beyond the bay, out on the sea, came flashes of light. They were followed by banging noises.

Brian, startled, sat up, only to have Shad haul him down.

Again the bursts of light came. Again the banging.

Shad pulled himself partway up, trying to see what was happening. Kinlow and the two men ran along the walkway and hurried out onto the dock. At the far end they stood and looked toward the sea.

More flashes of light. More banging.

"Gunshots," whispered Shad. "Someone's out there trying to catch them." He was sure it was Sheraton, and he felt annoyed. Why was Sheraton wasting his time, when Kinlow—the important one—was here on the island?

But after that there were no more flashes or sounds of shooting.

Kinlow and his men remained beneath the dock light, watching, talking quietly.

"Got to get closer," Shad whispered to Brian.

Now completely in the open, the two boys began to crawl toward the dock. Out in the bay the channel bell rang, a single stroke, then was silent.

The boys stopped.

"Who is it?" asked Brian.

Shad put a finger to his lips.

It was at least five more minutes before anything else happened. Then the channel bell rang again, one loud clang followed by two short strokes. It was the smugglers' signal that they were coming in.

The three men at the end of the dock began to move toward shore. As they did, a man came running from the opposite direction, and passed them. When that man reached the end of the dock, he turned the kerosene lamp off.

By the light of the moon the incoming boat appeared. It was much larger than Shad had remembered from the week before. Silver-colored, ghost-like, its motors rhythmically throbbing, its high prow loomed like a gigantic empty face.

Slowly, carefully, it slipped toward the dock.

"Bit more!" a voice from the boat called out.

Someone jumped from the boat to the dock. A squeaking sound came as the boat shoved against the wooden pilings.

"All fast!"

Instantly the boat came alive. Like seeds popping from a pod, men sprang from belowdecks. They leaped to the dock. Sounds of unloading, men working very fast. Cases were lowered to the dock. Shad strained to see exactly what they were unloading, trying to figure out if the cases were any different from those he had seen in Kinlow's house. But the only thing he could sense clearly was how many there were, many more, at least, than the last time.

And then Shad and Brian heard Bennett's truck, loud and raucous, crawling along the beach. One look back and Shad realized they were directly in its path.

"Come on!" Shad whispered. He grabbed Brian's arm. Brian scrambled after him. Crouching low, they ran up the beach, out of the way.

The truck clattered closer, seemingly picking up speed. Its headlights came on. Instantly, the boys were illuminated.

"There!" shouted someone. "There he is!"

Blinded by the glare, Shad sensed that people were all about them, that they were completely surrounded.

"Brian!" Shad cried. He reached for his brother, but touched nothing. Whirling around, he tried to see where he was, to get the light out of his eyes. Brian had vanished. All Shad could see were men rushing at him from all sides.

Shad began to run. A tall figure appeared before him. Lowering his head, Shad plunged, hitting the man hard. The man cried out, rolled away. Someone else reached out and held Shad's arm, pulling him down. Momentarily they struggled on the sand, but Shad was able to pull himself free and leap up. Finding his balance, he looked frantically again for his brother. "Brian!" he shouted.

"Here!" came a call. It wasn't Brian's voice, but Shad spun about anyway.

It was Bennett. Before Shad could dodge, Bennett took hold of him. Shad felt himself yanked off his feet. "Get out of here!" roared Bennett in his ear. "Get!" Shad found himself hurled out of the circle of men.

Staggering, he fell to his knees. Out of the brightness another large form came toward him. With a quick movement, Shad rolled away, got to his feet, and began to run wildly. He tripped on the wooden walkway, regained his balance, then ran between two houses.

"Stop him!" came a cry from behind. "He's the one I want! Get him! Get that one!" Shad recognized the voice: Kinlow.

Once past the row of Front Street houses, Shad broke from the paths and began to cut across the island in the valleys of the dunes. As he ran, he looked back over his shoulder. In the moonlight he could make out dark forms coming after him. He ran faster.

All he could think of was Brian. What had happened to him? Shad wanted to go back and find his brother. Brian needed him. But he was afraid to return to the beach.

Shad continued to move across the island, trying to decide which was the best way to go. Had Bennett helped him get away? He thought he had, but wasn't sure. Would Bennett help Brian? He didn't know that either. Who could he go to for help? Sheraton. He had to get to Sheraton!

Exhausted from running, Shad flopped down on the sand, keeping a watch to the bay side of the island while his breathing slowed to normal. The moonlight was bright enough for him to make out men prowling about, searching for him. There were a lot of men looking.

Shad began to wonder what had happened. The way Bennett's truck had come up, its lights suddenly blazing, someone yelling "There he is!" . . . The more he thought about it, the more convinced he was that they had known he was going to be there. A trap.

It made him feel weak all over.

As he lay back on the sand, Shad heard the bursting racket of Bennett's truck. That meant the cases had been loaded. The truck was moving on.

What was he to do about Brian?

The truck was going to Kinlow's house. If they had Brian, they would take him there. And Shad had to be sure the liquor was put into the house anyway. He would go there too.

Sometimes Shad walked, sometimes he ran. The sound of Bennett's truck came and went. It confused him. At times it sounded as if it was headed for a different place than he was. Yet he was sure it was going north, toward Kinlow's house, the way he was going. Where else could it go?

Kinlow's house sat in the moonlight, clearly deserted. No lights were on. The gate in the fence wasn't even closed.

Shad lay down behind some dune grass and waited for the truck. Once it arrived he would find some way to get Brian free.

But the longer he waited, the more puzzled he became. Why wasn't Bennett's truck there? He couldn't even hear the engine anymore. He listened intently to the silence. And then, with a sense of shock, he suddenly understood: the truck had gone directly to the marsh ferry landing.

Slowly, Shad got up, staring at the deserted house. He walked toward the gate, paused momentarily, then passed through. The front door was partly open. When he put a hand to it, it swung in.

Shad stepped into the house. Moonlight streamed through the open door. There was more than enough light for him to see that everything was different than it had been before. Furniture was pushed to one side. The doors to the other rooms were open.

With four steps Shad was at the door to the room where the liquor had been stored. Without even looking, he knew what he would find. One glance proved him right: all the liquor was gone.

Upset, confused, Shad made his way out of the house. He stood in the empty front yard, trying to figure out what had happened.

The gunshots at sea, he decided, must have been an attempt by Sheraton's people to stop the smugglers. That had failed. He'd seen that for himself. The boat had come in. But apparently the gunfire had alarmed Kinlow. Kinlow must have decided not to take chances, but to get rid of the evidence. He had gone straight to the ferry; he would ship the liquor to the mainland right away. But when, and how, had Kinlow moved the bottles that had been in the house?

Then Shad remembered about Brian. Kinlow—if he had him—must have taken him to the ferry.

Shad began to run hard across the island.

15

AS SHAD APPROACHED THE MARSH SIDE OF THE IS-
land, he heard the sound of Bennett's truck starting up.
For a moment he stopped. Then he ran faster, until at
last he was climbing the dune that overlooked the ferry
landing. Bennett's truck, headlights on, was grinding
slowly away down the beach.

On the beach, some fifteen yards up from the water,
was a pyramid of wooden cases, the cases stacked seven
and eight high. It was the smuggled liquor.

There were men on the beach, too. A few had sat

down on cases, while others walked about. A couple of them stood on either side of the mountain of boxes like guards. Shad counted eleven men in all.

Despite the bright moonlight, Shad couldn't see exactly who the men were. And at first he thought some of them were carrying sticks. When he saw the metallic glint, however, he realized that the "sticks" were rifles.

One figure that he had not noticed at first caught his attention. He was smaller than the others, and sitting on one of the cases, still and isolated. Brian.

At once Shad's anger and anxiety returned. He had to get Brian away.

One of the men around the cases walked away from the others. He moved slowly in Shad's direction. For a moment Shad even thought the man was coming right to him, but halfway to the base of the dune the man stopped and looked back. Shad recognized him then. Kinlow.

"Joe!" Kinlow called out.

The men around the cases looked up.

"Joe!" Kinlow called a second time.

A figure detached itself from the others and began to move toward Kinlow. Shad tried to think who "Joe" might be. He didn't know anyone by that name. But there was something about the way this man moved that seemed familiar.

Kinlow, not waiting for "Joe" to catch up, walked even closer to where Shad was hiding. The man called Joe trudged through the soft sand after him. Close to Kinlow he stopped, looked up, and, with a swift flip of his head, tossed the hair out of his eyes. It was Mr. Sheraton!

Unwilling to believe what he himself was seeing, Shad rose up to his knees and stared. But there was no mistake. The man called Joe was Sheraton. What was Sheraton doing there? Shad guessed that he must have been captured, just as Brian had been.

"What do you want?" Shad heard Sheraton say.

"I need to talk to you," said Kinlow, taking a few more steps up the dune. "Privately."

Sheraton drew closer.

Then Kinlow said, "You're going to have to get Jefferson to move faster."

"Can't," said Sheraton right away. "He's overloaded as it is."

Kinlow took his watch from his pocket and squinted at it. "We'll be here all night at this rate."

"It was your decision to clear out," said Sheraton. "Not mine. Anyway, no one is going to bother us. It doesn't matter."

Shad felt a wave of nausea. *Sheraton had tricked him.* He tried to push away his sense of panic.

"Of course it matters!" snapped Kinlow. "I'm telling you, we have to load more at a time."

"That boat can't take it."

"It'll have to."

"You're too nervous," suggested Sheraton.

"That other Faherty boy is still out there," said Kinlow. "I don't like it. I don't know what he's up to. Do you? Didn't you tell him to come here?"

"You were supposed to grab him on the other side," said Sheraton. "I was sure he'd be watching, and he was.

You're the one who let him slip through your fingers. And if you hadn't tried to bully him, you wouldn't have had to worry about him in the first place."

"I think I know what's best," snapped Kinlow.

"Sure you do. That kid managed to learn just about everything. He even got into your house. Leaving the back door open . . . it's a wonder he didn't learn about me. Don't worry. He's a kid. He thinks I'm with the government. Besides, he's probably scared off by now. If he were coming here he would have been here at ten, as we agreed. Why don't you just forget about him?"

"I intend to catch him," said Kinlow.

"Come on. Nothing is going to happen. They're just kids." And, turning away, Sheraton headed back down toward the liquor cases.

For a moment Kinlow stayed behind. Then he followed.

Shad felt sick, sick with anger and betrayal. He'd been made a fool of. He'd been tricked. He'd been cheated. And he wasn't the only one who had been hurt, either. By doing what he'd done he managed to get Brian caught. Now he had to get Brian free—no matter who was there, no matter how many guns they had.

For the moment he didn't care about anything else.

The men down along the beach began to stir. At first Shad couldn't tell why. Then he heard what they must have heard—sounds coming from the marsh. Mr. Jefferson's ferry was coming in.

Some twenty feet from the shore, the boat stopped. The men on the beach had already become busy, each one picking up a case and wading into the water to the waiting boat.

"Come on, boy," someone yelled to Brian. "Out of the way!"

Shad looked over at his brother. Brian had sprung up from the case on which he'd been sitting and had moved away a few paces.

"Move!" the man barked. Brian edged farther away. He was now several yards from the pile of cases and the busily working men. No one was paying attention to him. Even Sheraton was loading. Kinlow, at the water's edge, was giving orders.

Shad saw that if Brian ran, right then, he would get away. Once, twice, he thought he saw Brian make a tentative move, only to stop and just stand there. "Come on!" Shad cried silently to his brother. "Come on!" But Brian didn't budge. Shad understood. Brian was too scared to move. Shad would have to help.

The dune behind which Shad was hiding was shaped like a half moon, both ends curving in toward the water. Ducking down behind the dune, Shad ran some fifty feet, then climbed up to take another look. He was now on the other side of Brian, but also some twenty feet closer.

Brian hadn't moved.

Shad picked up a pebble and threw it. It landed close to his brother, but Brian didn't even seem to notice.

Shad threw another, harder. This time the stone went

too far, hitting one of the cases with a sharp crack. Brian looked up. None of the men did.

Still Brian didn't turn in Shad's direction.

Shad picked up a third stone and threw it, aiming it right at Brian. It hit him on the leg. Brian jumped and spun about to see where the stone had come from.

Realizing that he had to take a chance, Shad stood up, showing himself for a split second. Then, just as quickly, he dropped back down.

Brian stood straighter and took a step toward the dune. Shad knew then that his brother had seen him. But then, cautiously, Brian turned back to look at the working men. Once more, he looked over to where Shad was.

"Run!" Shad screamed silently, trying desperately to figure out some way to make his brother understand what he had to do.

But Brian only stood where he was, twisting his hands together, a picture of caution. He took two tentative steps toward Shad, only to stop once more.

One of the men—Shad recognized him as an islander—passed close to Brian on his way to pick up a box. As he bent over to lift it, he noticed Brian standing by, gazing dumbly at him. The man picked up the box, looked at Brian again, then put the box down. Quickly, he looked around, then suddenly reached out and gave Brian a shove, pushing him away from the pile of cases.

Still Brian stood motionless, as if not fully comprehending what had been done. The man made a quick, exasperated motion, waving his arm, pointing.

Brian understood. He spun about and raced toward the dune and Shad.

As Brian made off, another man straightened up. "Hey, stop!" he called.

Two more men turned around. "The kid's skipping!" someone yelled.

At the water's edge, a case in his arms, Sheraton spun about. Hurriedly he put the box down. "Get him!" he cried.

At once, two men began to lumber after Brian.

Brian, meanwhile, had pumped up the dune and flung himself over the top, gasping, crying, clutching at Shad.

Shad grabbed him, but gave Brian no time to rest. "Come on!" he cried, and hauled his brother to his feet. Brian, half running, half stumbling, allowed himself to be led.

· · 16

THERE WAS NO TIME TO THINK. THE MEN FOLLOW-
ing Brian would be over the top of the dune and onto
them in a matter of seconds. Shad simply ran. All but
carrying Brian, he ran down along the valley. Brian
tripped and tumbled, bringing Shad down into the sand
with him.

The moment they hit the ground, Brian struggled to
get up. Shad pressed him down. "Don't move!" he
hissed. With his arm across his brother's back, he held
him flat.

The two men who had been chasing Brian came up over the crest of the dune and paused. The dune cast a shadow, so the boys' footprints could not be easily seen. Hardly pausing, the men dove into the valley and went up over the next dune. In seconds they were out of sight.

Still Shad waited. Another man—Shad thought it might be Sheraton—came over the top of the first dune. Two others followed. They stood for a moment, then plunged after the first two men.

"Okay," Shad whispered to Brian when the last of the men had disappeared.

Brian, trembling, sat up. Immediately he buried his face against Shad's chest, sobbing. Shad wrapped his arms around him. Brian kept trying to rub the tears from his face, but only succeeded in covering his face with patches of sand.

"You okay?" Shad asked when Brian's crying had eased.

Brian sniffed deeply.

"Don't worry," said Shad. "You got away."

Brian looked up. "I though you said that Mr. Sheraton was your friend. He works for Kinlow too!"

"He tricked me."

"That sure wasn't Sheraton out there trying to catch them, either."

"Who was it?"

"They don't know. But they think you had something to do with it," said Brian. "At least Kinlow thinks so. He's so mad. He said if he ever caught you he'd teach you a lesson you'd never forget. Said he gave you a warning, and now he was going to do something about it."

Shad wondered if that meant doing something to his parents too.

"Can we go home?" Brian asked.

Shad quickly shook his head. "The ones chasing you, they're between us and home. Anyway, that's the first place they'll look for us. We can't go there."

"They going to do anything to Ma or Dad?"

"I don't know."

"Shad," said Brian, the tears beginning to flow again, "what're we going to do?"

"I don't know," said Shad again. "You have to give me time to think."

After a while Brian asked, "What are you thinking?"

"The mainland," answered Shad.

"Mainland?" repeated Brian.

"We could get help there."

"Who?"

"Police, maybe. Someone."

"Isn't there anyone closer?"

"Who?"

Brian looked at his brother as if he were crazy. "Where're you going to get a boat?" he wanted to know. "Steal it?"

Shad shook his head. "Can't get a boat. All the boats are on the bay side. There'll be people there. People looking for us. Look here, it'll be really low tide in an hour. It's going down right now, isn't it? It's shallow."

"So what?"

"Well, we'll walk."

"To the *mainland*?"

Shad nodded, yes.

"Across the marsh?" cried Brian.

"Can we get home?" asked Shad.

"Guess not."

"Soon as we try to get a boat, sure enough, someone will be on to us, right?"

"I suppose."

"And we don't have the time, anyway. Besides, what if Kinlow does do something, like going after Ma and Dad? Then what? We can't just do nothing, can we?"

Brian was speechless.

"See," said Shad. "We *have* to go there. There's nothing else to do. And the only way to go is by walking. There's no other way."

"I can't," said Brian in a voice so small Shad could hardly hear it.

"You came tonight, didn't you?" asked Shad. "They even caught you but you got away."

Brian shook his head. "I'll be too scared."

"No, you won't."

"I was before, when they caught me."

"You got free," Shad said firmly. "And the tide's going down. We can go from dry spot to dry spot."

"People get drowned trying that," said Brian.

"Well, we won't."

"Where would we start?"

"Someplace they can't see us."

"They have an awful lot of boxes," remarked Brian. "I heard them say they'd be there till morning. They're taking them all."

"How come?"

"They're not going to come back for a while. Because of what you did."

"Me?"

"That's what they said."

"I don't believe it."

"They said it. Shad?"

"What?"

"If they're going anyway, if they're going for good, maybe we don't have to do anything."

"And let Kinlow just get away?" Shad stood up. "I'm going. You coming?"

"What if it gets too hard and I want to go back?"

"Don't worry. We'll get there."

"You really think so?"

"Think I want to drown myself?"

"All right," said Brian. He got up slowly.

Shad began to lead the way to the beach. They walked in silence, heading south from the ferry landing area. Sometimes Brian skipped to keep up. And now and again he would reach out to touch Shad, reminding him that he was there.

From the crest of the dune that bordered the beach they looked out over the marsh. The black water was slate smooth, almost glassy, broken only by the salt-hay islands. In the light of the moon, the grass was pale green. Some islands were just clumps of grass, no more than a few feet across. Others, rounding out of the water, were true islands. Beyond the marsh, the mainland was nothing but a glow over the horizon.

"How far is it?" asked Brian, his voice hushed.

"About two miles. See, the tide's still going out. We won't even get our knees wet."

Nervously, Brian chewed his lip, staring out over the marsh.

"Come on," urged Shad, and he slid down the dune and began to walk toward the water. Brian followed. At the water's edge they paused. Shad stepped into the water first. It was cool. He went out a few feet, then turned. Brian was still on the shore.

"Come on!" hissed Shad.

"How long do you think it'll take?"

"Not long. Not if we get going and move fast. Come on."

"Okay," said Brian, taking a few tentative steps forward.

"Just stay close. I'll feel out the firm bottom."

"Okay," said Brian again. He drew close enough to Shad to touch his overalls.

They began to move in earnest. Very quickly, the water reached over Shad's ankles. The black bottom became so stirred up that when he looked down he couldn't see his toes.

Shad moved toward the first clump of grass. But when the water didn't reach any higher than his ankles, he passed it by. "Long as it's shallow," he said, "it'll be faster going straight on through."

They kept going.

"It isn't so bad," said Brian after a while. He sounded greatly relieved. Still, he kept reaching out, touching Shad.

Shad pushed forward, his feet splashing with every step. Once, twice, he suddenly sank into a hole of black ooze, but for the most part the bottom held firm.

Shad stopped when the water reached mid-calf. Brian was so close behind he bumped into Shad. Together they looked back. The sand of Lucker's Island seemed to be a shimmery white.

"We've come a whole lot," said Brian.

"Not bad."

"Guess not," said Brian. His voice kept getting stronger.

"Come on," said Shad.

They went on.

17

BEHIND THEM, LUCKER'S ISLAND HAD BECOME nothing but a ribbon. Above them, the moon was high. Before them, the marsh seemed endless.

Shad had no particular direction in mind. He was simply aiming for the vague glow that crowned the mainland. He moved forward. He skirted the grass islands. He avoided looking back.

"Have we come halfway?" asked Brian.

"I don't know. Just keep going. If we don't hurry they'll be all cleared out. There'll be nothing to catch them with." Just the thought made Shad want to try to move faster.

The water had reached Shad's knees, Brian's thighs.

"Wait up!" cried Brian. He had fallen a little way behind.

Shad stopped. Brian sloshed up as fast as he could. "I think I heard something," he said. "Voices." He was whispering.

Shad stood motionless, listening. Sure enough, a man's voice floated across the still marsh.

"Good thing it's so bright," the voice said. It was hard to know just where it was coming from.

Then came a churning sound.

"What is it?" Brian whispered, his voice full of alarm.

"Mr. Jefferson," said Shad softly. "The ferryboat."

Shad stood stock-still, trying to decide which direction the boat was coming from. Though the churning grew louder, the island prevented them from seeing anything.

"Come on," whispered Shad. Grabbing hold of Brian's hand, he moved around one of the salt-hay hillocks. "Squat down," he said. Brian did as he was told.

The marsh ferry drew closer.

"That Faherty boy, the young one, he got away," a voice said.

"Good," said another. "I didn't like holding him."

"He tried to bust things up, didn't he?"

"Kinlow said he and his brother were trying to get the Coast Guard."

"Not the young one. It's the other one, that Shad, who was making the problems."

"Well, Kinlow says he'll take care of him. But he's planning to clear out for a while. Just in case."

"Kinlow likes doing things his way."

"He's not easy. That's for sure."

Shad kept pressing his hand to Brian's back to keep him low. He himself looked up. Mr. Jefferson's boat was not ten feet away. It was in the channel directly opposite, on the other side of the island. Instantly, Shad ducked. But he wasn't quick enough.

"Hey," called someone. "I saw a face. Someone's out here!"

Shad dropped down lower. Only his head was above water. Brian did the same, his chin stretched up.

"You crazy?" came Mr. Jefferson's voice. "No one's going to be out here."

"A ghost, then."

The churning stopped.

"Where'd you see it?"

"Over there."

"Maybe one of the kids," said another voice.

"Here?"

"I'm telling you, I saw something. It sure looked like a face."

"Show me where," said Mr. Jefferson.

"There, where I'm pointing."

The paddle wheel began to churn again, but not as fast as before.

Shad, in an effort to get even lower, swallowed water. Trying not to cough, he jerked his head up, and stared right at Mr. Jefferson. For the briefest second, their eyes met.

Quickly Mr. Jefferson turned away. "No one here," he said.

"Try the other side of that grass."

"I told you," said Mr. Jefferson. "No one was there."

"Sure looked like it."

"Full moon plays tricks."

The paddle wheel beat loudly. Waves washed against the boys' faces.

"Come on. Kinlow is going to give us a hard time if we're late."

Slowly, the marsh boat moved away.

"Okay," whispered Shad. He stood up.

Brian, shaking, also stood. They were both thoroughly soaked and cold.

"We better go this way," said Shad. Not wanting Brian to see how agitated he was, he began to lead to the right.

"Shad?" said Brian after they had been going for a while.

"What?"

"I'm tired."

Shad looked at his brother, then searched for a place to get out of the water.

"Over there," he said, pointing to a round of grass. When he reached it, he pulled himself up, then turned to help Brian. The grass cut and stuck to their arms.

"How far have we come?" Brian wanted to know.

Shad stood up and looked about in a wide circle. They were in an area that seemed no different from any other through which they had passed—except that Shad could no longer see Lucker's Island. The mainland, with its soft, glowing light, seemed no closer.

"I don't know," he admitted.

"Think it's halfway now?" asked Brian.

The bright light of the moon had made the stars fade. Beyond, the black sky seemed to be part of the marsh. It all seemed endless. Shad tried not to show what he was feeling and thinking, his increasing confusion about the right direction, his sense that the water was getting deeper, his worry about Brian.

"Maybe," said Brian carefully, "maybe we should go back." He stole a glance up at Shad.

"We'll get there," said Shad, as much to encourage himself as Brian.

"I'm glad they didn't catch us," said Brian.

"Come on," said Shad. He worked his way down from the hillock, back into the chilly water. Brian hesitated. "Come on," urged Shad.

Reluctantly, Brian returned to the water. "Which way?" he asked.

"Toward the light."

Shad began to wade forward again. The water was almost up to his waist. Underfoot, the bottom was becoming thicker, softer.

It was Shad who slipped first.

He had been walking on what seemed a firm bottom.

At the very next step his foot sank deeply, as if it were being pulled from below. He sprawled headfirst into the water. Splashing about, he gradually worked his way back to where Brian was standing, too frightened to move.

Shad's face and arms were streaked with black mud. "Bottom's too soft there," he said. "Better go this way."

But there was no other way to go. No matter which way they turned, they sank into soft, sucking mud. At last Shad decided they should try to edge their way around the morass. He started again.

"Shad?"

"What?"

"We can't go that way. That's where Mr. Jefferson was."

"He's gone."

"Please!"

Standing still, Shad tried to decide which way to go. He just didn't know.

Brian watched him carefully. "Don't you think we should go back?"

Shad shook his head.

"We're going to drown."

"Stop talking so much!" Shad cried. Brian opened his mouth, then closed it. "Come on," said Shad gently. "We'll make it."

Again Shad tried to move forward. Instantly the bottom caught him. He sank at least a foot. He pushed on anyway. Brian, clinging to him now, half swam, half walked. The clutching mud made each step an effort. In the time it had taken to cover ten feet before, Shad could only move three.

After a while Shad stopped, exhausted. "Be better if we went from island to island," he said. "Be easier."

Brian, too upset, too numb, could only nod.

Shad searched out the biggest mound of dry island he could see. It was about twelve feet from where they were. Keeping Brian close, he moved toward it, foot by foot. The ground began to firm. When he was close enough, Shad reached forward, grasped the salt-hay stalks, attempted to pull himself toward the land. The stalks snapped.

Recovering, Shad adjusted his footing, then reached out again and gathered more grass in his hands. This time it held. He was able to pull himself onto the hillock. He turned and hauled Brian up after him.

They rested.

When Shad was ready and thought Brian had had enough time, he stood up and picked the next place to go, repeating the whole process.

After the sixth hillock they were both too tired to move. Their skin itched where black mud had caked and clotted. Shad's hands stung, cut by the grass spikes. His feet had been cut by shells. The mainland's glow seemed no closer. Shad had the terrible feeling they were lost.

"Shad," said Brian, his voice trembling, "I can't do any more."

"We're halfway," said Shad, not knowing if it was

true. "If we went back it would be just as far as going on. Anyway, we can't stop here."

"Why not?"

"We can't, that's all."

"Why *not?*" insisted Brian.

Shad took a breath. "The tide will turn, that's why not. It's low now, extra low, isn't it?"

"I suppose," said Brian.

"Well then, what's the opposite? It'll be extra high, won't it? All the islands will be under water. We can't swim it, can we? We have to move."

Shad didn't even wait for Brian to respond. He clambered back down into the water, pulling Brian after him. Once more he led the way.

18

THE BOTTOM GREW WORSE. THEY HAD TO STOP after every step, not just to get their strength back, but to help each other. The water between hillocks was up to Brian's chest.

It seemed darker, too. Shad looked up. He had no idea how long they had been going, but the moon had begun to drop.

They stood motionless in the water.

"How long we been going?" Brian wanted to know.

"An hour, maybe," said Shad.

"Seems like more than that. How much farther?"

"Not much."

"We going to get there?"

"Sure."

Brian rubbed his hands across his face, smearing it even more. "Shad?"

"What?"

"I don't feel like going anymore. . . . Are you cold?"

"A bit," said Shad, not wanting to admit how cold he truly felt.

"I'm a lot," said Brian.

"Look," said Shad, "when I find the next real high place, we'll rest a good while. Just a little farther, okay?"

"Okay," said Brian. He sounded sleepy.

After a few more steps, feeling more tired himself than ever, Shad had to stop and wait again. He began to wonder if they would ever reach land. He closed his eyes. He felt dizzy.

And he heard a sound.

At first he wasn't certain what it was, or even if it *was* something. But it kept coming, a soft slapping sound. It would come, then stop, only to come again.

"You hear that?" whispered Shad.

"What?" asked Brian. Instantly alarmed, he snapped out of his drowsiness.

"That."

The sound came again. It sounded like oars.

They strained to listen.

For a moment there was silence; then the sounds came again, now distinct splashes. Brian's eyes grew wide.

Trying to push away his own panic, Shad said, in a low voice, "Let's get over there." He pointed to a grass island. It was a small one, one they had already passed. Nevertheless, Shad moved toward it, holding tightly to Brian's arm. They couldn't move very fast, and between steps they listened.

"That's oars," said Brian.

"Get to the grass," Shad whispered urgently.

When they reached the island, they managed to work themselves up silently. They lay low, trying to make themselves invisible. Then, cautiously, Shad lifted his head.

At first he couldn't tell which way to look. But when the splashes came again he was able to figure just where they were coming from: the mainland side.

"Who is it?" whispered Brian.

Shad lifted himself slightly and saw a long rowboat. At first he counted six men in it. All of them were dressed in dark clothing. Then he saw a seventh man in the stern.

"*Who is it?*" Brian barely breathed. This was enough to tell Shad how terrified he was. Shad's own heart was racing. He touched Brian's mouth to make him keep still.

The boat pulled closer. The oar strokes came easily, carefully, a long moment apart.

"Kinlow?" whispered Brian. His teeth were chattering.

Again Shad lifted himself. The rowers all had their backs to him. Only the man in the stern was facing their direction, and Shad couldn't yet make him out clearly.

A few more oar strokes.

As the men pulled, Shad could hear their breathing,

and the cutting swish of the boat as it slid through the grasses.

Shad lifted himself even higher. Now he could see the man in the stern clearly.

It was Mr. Nevill.

Shad just stared, hoping his eyes were fooling him. But it was Nevill. Horrified, he turned to Brian.

Brian, trying to see who it was, got up on all fours. Suddenly his face lit up, and he turned to Shad with great relief. "It's Mr. Nevill," he said loudly.

In a flash Shad realized that he had never told Brian about Mr. Nevill, who he really was. "Get down!" he hissed.

But Brian was not to be held back. "Here!" he cried out. "Mr. Nevill! We're here!"

Shad tried to pull him down, but it was too late. Brian, all but hysterical with joy, was waving his arms, calling, "Here! Help!"

Shad sprang up. The boat was no more than ten yards away. The rowers had all swung around to look in their direction. Some were half standing. Shad could see Mr. Nevill, tallest, in the stern.

Almost instantly, Nevill sat down. Shad heard him call, "Pull!" The men at the oars responded, swinging the boat sharply to the right, heading directly for the boys.

Grabbing hold of Brian, Shad leaped into the water. Brian tried to yank away, but Shad, his grip on his brother unrelenting, began to struggle fiercely through the water.

Shad glanced back over his shoulder. The boat was coming after them. Its prow loomed high; a curl of wash sprayed back from its bow. A man was standing up. He seemed gigantic. "There they are!" he cried. He pointed right at the boys.

The oars slapped hard at the water.

Desperately, Shad looked for an island. He spotted one and struggled toward it, still pulling at the flailing Brian. He clutched at the grass. Brian, trying to get out of Shad's grasp, broke free, only to sink. Shad spun about, lifted him, all but threw him on the island, then scrambled up after him. Brian, choking, spat out water.

"There!" came a cry from the boat. The oars swished.

Shad turned to Brian. His brother was doubled over, holding his belly, weeping wildly. "Nevill's with Kinlow," Shad yelled at him. "You hear me? He's with Kinlow!" Brian, understanding at last, looked up at Shad with a face of utter defeat.

Shad whirled around to face the boat. He had to save Brian. Hoping to divert the men's attention, he dove, headfirst, off the island and into the channel.

Down into the black muck he went. Kicking for all he was worth, he sought the bottom. His fingers clutched everywhere, trying to find something to cling to, something to keep him down. All he felt was slime . . . nothing to hold to. Even as he groped in the muck, his chest began to feel the pain. He felt as if he were going to burst.

Unable to stay below a second longer, Shad shot up to the surface, sputtering, waving his arms. Even as he did, he felt a hand drop onto his head and grasp his hair. He shook his head violently, trying to pull loose, in one last effort to keep free.

"Brian!" he screamed. "Get away. Go!" More hands reached down and clutched at him. He felt himself lifted up bodily, then rolled over the side of the boat and dropped into the bottom.

He was caught.

19

SPENT OF ENERGY, SHAD LAY IN THE BOTTOM OF
the boat. He was filthy with slime. He kept spitting out
brackish water. He could feel that the boat was not moving, but rocking gently in place. From somewhere he
heard a whimpering sound, and knew that it must be
Brian. They had caught him too.

Shad struggled to sit up, but something was holding
him back. He opened his eyes. Mr. Nevill was looking
down at him, a hand on his shoulder.

"You all right?" Nevill asked.

Shad closed his eyes again, not wanting to see, much less talk. He lay back, feeling a vast heaviness, the weight of his own failure. Dizziness swept over him.

When he opened his eyes again there were more faces looking down.

"Your brother is fine," said Nevill.

Shad clenched his teeth.

"What are you doing out here?" asked Nevill. "Do you have any idea where you are? If you'd gone much farther you'd have reached the end of the marsh and deep water. You've come quite a way." He smiled. But as he saw the intensity of Shad's look, the smile faded. "You weren't trying to reach the mainland, were you?" Shad said nothing. "You should have come along with me when I asked you to."

Shad gazed up at Nevill. "You're with Kinlow," he said.

"Is that what you think?" asked Nevill. His face grew solemn.

"You didn't have to come into the bay," said Shad. "You broke your motor yourself. And you were listening to Kinlow's messages. I watched you."

"That's true," said Nevill. "But you left out something important." He drew in one of the men who was looking on. "Can you read this?" he asked Shad.

Reluctantly, Shad turned and looked where Nevill was pointing. On the man's jacket sleeve was an eagle insignia. Arching over it were the words, "U.S. Coast Guard."

Shad opened his eyes wide.

"Since you know so much," said Nevill, "you might have guessed that too. In fact, I thought you had."

Shad pushed himself up to a sitting position and looked at the other men. All six of them had on Coast Guard uniforms. Then he saw Brian. He was at the far end of the boat, wrapped in a blanket. His eyes were closed.

"He's asleep," said Nevill.

Shad turned back to Nevill. "Just because you're Coast Guard doesn't mean anything. You could still be with Kinlow."

"I'm not."

"Why did you want me to go with you today?"

"I knew what you were up to. I didn't want you to get hurt."

"How did you know?"

"From Kinlow's messages. He knew you were trying to catch him, get him sent to jail. Sheraton told him. The fact is, Shad, it was Sheraton who set this whole operation up. The island was his discovery, his idea. The two worked together. Quite a pair."

Shad let this sink in. "He didn't *discover* the island," he said bitterly. "There were lots of people here already."

"I guess they forgot that, didn't they?"

"Was that you out on the ocean before, trying to catch them?" Shad suddenly asked. "We heard gunshots."

Nevill nodded. "I thought I could catch them with their liquor before they reached the island. It would have been better that way. I still don't know how many island people work for Kinlow. And I don't really want to get involved with them." His face took on a less serious look. "For a while I even thought you were with him. That time you caught me poking around his house, you scared me off. The point is, I still want to try and get them. I just hope they've still got the stuff." He nodded toward the island. "You have to catch them with it."

"That's what Sheraton told me."

"He should know."

Shad tried to think it all through. "How do I know you're telling me the truth now?" he asked softly.

Nevill considered. "Guess you'll have to take a chance."

"Is Nevill your real name?" said Shad.

Briefly, Nevill paused. Then he said, "No."

"What is it?"

"Costello. Anthony Costello. How's that? Believe me now?"

"I want to."

Costello smiled. "Try. Because I need you to tell me some things. What's happened? Why were you out here? What were you trying to do?"

Shad closed his eyes, trying to decide whether he should trust Costello. He wanted to. He looked at the man again.

"Try," Costello repeated.

Gradually, haltingly, but with a growing sense of relief, Shad told Costello everything that had happened from the time he'd broken away from him that morning. He described the scene on the beach. "They've got a whole lot this time," said Shad. "They're trying to clear it all off. If we hurry, maybe we could catch them."

"You don't give up, do you?"

Shad shook his head.

"Well," said Costello. "We'll have to see."

He returned to the stern of the boat while his six men took up their oars. Shad took a place near Brian, who was still sleeping.

The boat went forward swiftly, moving very quietly, twisting and turning among the grass islands. Shad began to realize how far he and Brian had come.

From time to time Costello stood and scanned the horizon. Gradually, the long, low form of Lucker's Island, its white beaches glowing in the last of the night, revealed itself.

To the west a banner of stars spread across the sky.

Costello directed the rowers to the southern part of the island, well away from the ferry landing.

"You know about Mr. Jefferson's boat, don't you?" asked Shad.

Costello nodded.

"Mr. Jefferson helped us get away. He saw us out in the marsh, but he didn't let on."

"Good."

"They have rifles," said Shad.

"So do we."

"Kinlow has his own pistol."

"You don't have to worry," said Costello. "When we go for them you'll stay behind. You won't be in any danger of being hurt."

"I want to go with you," said Shad right away, dismayed that he might be left behind because Costello thought he was afraid.

"Up to a point," Costello returned. "Now, get your brother up. We're coming in."

There was a grating sound as the boat slid up to the shore. While the six men shipped their oars and leaped overboard, Costello helped both boys out. Brian, still groggy, stayed close by Shad's side. They watched as the men, pulling the boat, ran it high on the beach.

"We'll want to come up behind them," Costello explained to Shad. "That way the water will be at their backs—there'll be no place for them to go."

"You going to arrest all of them?" asked Shad. "Kinlow made the other people work for him. They don't like him either. You can ask them."

"We're only interested in Kinlow, the two men with him, and Sheraton. I don't care about the rest."

"Bennett helped me too," added Shad.

Costello smiled. "I told you, it's those four we want." He turned to Brian. "You okay?"

Brian nodded, gazing at Costello and the other men. Shad could see that his brother didn't understand what was happening, but he didn't want to take the time to explain.

Costello took the lead, allowing Shad and Brian to stay close. They moved inland over the dunes. Each of the Coast Guard men carried a rifle. Costello held a pistol in his hand.

Whatever exhaustion Shad had felt was gone. When

he looked over his shoulder and saw the men following, he felt strong, excited. Now, at last, truly, they were going to get Kinlow.

From time to time Shad scrambled up to the top of a dune and looked over the beaches. There was just enough light to see. After they had gone about three-quarters of a mile, he was able to make out the smugglers and the mound of cases, much smaller now.

Softly he called to Costello, who trotted up the dune and lay down beside him.

For a while Costello looked on silently. Then, giving a tug to Shad's arm, he moved back down the dune. Shad followed.

Costello called his men together. In a low voice he told them exactly what he had seen and explained his plans. He wanted to move quickly, before dawn broke. There wasn't much time.

Two of the men would continue northward, moving past the smugglers. Two others would also go northward, but would stop when they were directly opposite the ferry landing. Finally, the last two would move up, but would stay to the south of the smugglers. Costello would go with the middle group. Kinlow and the others would be surrounded.

Costello told them he would fire into the air: that would be their signal to move in. He reminded them that he wanted no one killed, or, if possible, even hurt.

"What about us?" piped up Brian. He was having trouble keeping his eyes open.

Costello put a hand on Brian's shoulder. "This part we

have to do alone. We can't be sure what will happen, or
what they'll do. I hope they'll just give up. But they
might try to get away, and they are armed. You've
helped a lot," he added before Shad could protest. "A
whole lot. But it'll be too dangerous for you. I want you
to go now."

"Can we?" Brian asked eagerly.

"Absolutely. Scoot."

Brian, delighted, took a few steps away, only to stop
when he realized that Shad wasn't moving.

"I want to help catch Kinlow," Shad said to Costello.

Costello shook his head. "Believe me, you already
have. You've done plenty."

"Come on," urged Brian.

Reluctantly, Shad moved toward his brother.

"I promise I'll come visit you later," said Costello. "I'll
tell you everything that happens. But we've got to hurry.
It'll be daylight soon." He turned to his six men. "Here
we go."

Without waiting for the boys to move away, the seven
began to walk northward.

Shad watched them go. He felt cheated. Catching
Kinlow was what he had wanted to do most of all. Now,
he couldn't even see it happen.

Brian tugged at Shad's hand, then started to walk
away. Slowly, Shad followed.

The two boys climbed out of the valley, then went
down the eastern side of the next dune. Once, twice,
Brian yawned. Abruptly, Shad stopped.

"What is it?" asked Brian.

"You go on. I'm going back."

"He said not to."

"I want to be there when they catch Kinlow."

Brian looked at his brother. "You sure?"

"Yeah."

Brian waited for a moment. Then he said, "I'm going," and immediately he began to run in the direction of home.

···20

SHAD WATCHED UNTIL BRIAN WAS OUT OF SIGHT. Then he turned and ran back up the dune they had just come down. Over the crest and down into the next valley he raced, certain that from the top of the next dune he'd be able to see the ferry landing and the capture of Kinlow.

There was a gunshot from the north. Instantly, Shad stopped. That, he was sure, was Costello's signal. But the next moment there came a whole series of shots one after the other, crackling like fireworks. Shad wondered what might be happening. Were the Coast Guard men shooting? Were the smugglers fighting back, trying to escape?

Even as Shad stood there, there was another fierce burst of gunshots and then yet another. Shad's heart sank. All that shooting had to mean that something had gone wrong, that Costello's plan wasn't working.

Keeping well below the crest of the dune that bordered the beach, Shad began to run again, this time toward the north, peering into the semidarkness.

Far to the east, a jagged cut of red light appeared, a wound in the dark. Above, the sky was turning a dull, dawn gray.

Through the murk ahead, Shad saw the silhouetted figure of a man appear. The man was coming toward Shad, but at a slant, heading deeper into the dune area, his jacket tails fluttering.

The man climbed the dune to Shad's right, went over the top and was gone.

Kinlow.

Shad's whole body tightened. His chest felt heavy, his mouth dry. He hurried up to the top of the dune, then looked in the direction from which Kinlow had come. No one was coming after him. Shad made up his mind in a second. He took off in the same direction Kinlow had gone.

He went down the side of the dune and then up another and looked about. Kinlow was two dunes over, running hard across the cut of light.

Shad took off after him, crossing two dunes. Atop the second he stopped again and watched.

Kinlow was still ahead, but suddenly much closer than Shad had thought he'd be. He kept looking back toward the area of the ferry landing, nervously smoothing his jacket. He moved a hand toward his neck, tugged at his collar.

Shad followed Kinlow's look. Where was Costello?

When Shad turned back toward the smuggler, he was running again, darting up and down the dunes, moving in and out of sight, heading toward the northern part of the island. And Shad began to understand why. Most of the empty houses were there. Kinlow was looking for a place to hide.

Reaching a high point, Kinlow stopped and looked about in a wide circle. The morning light, though still gray, was brightening. Shad, stopping too, just watched from two dunes away. It was then that Kinlow realized he had been followed. Across the distance that separated them, they faced each other.

Neither moved.

Suddenly Kinlow turned and hurried along the dune crest in full stride, once more dropping out of sight.

Shad, determined not to lose him, continued to follow. Again he saw him, only to watch him drop down behind yet another dune. Every time Kinlow disappeared, Shad's heart would beat hard. But the next moment he would spot him.

Shad kept running, staying low, dodging behind clumps of grass and bushes, moving up and down the sandy hills, trying to keep out of sight.

Ahead of him, Kinlow stumbled, his knees touching the ground. As he righted himself he glanced back over his shoulder.

Instantly, Shad dove below the crest of his own dune, then slowly raised himself to his knees and watched. Kinlow was sitting down, facing in Shad's direction, rubbing his left ankle.

Shad watched him intently, wishing that Costello and his men would appear. Momentarily he turned to look back toward the ferry landing. When he looked at Kinlow again, he realized that Kinlow had spotted him.

The next moment, Kinlow, struggling to his feet, had started to run again, heading north. But now he was limping badly. Shad leapt up and set off after him, no longer bothering to keep hidden. There were houses up ahead.

Kinlow staggered to a stop, almost falling. He turned toward Shad. "Keep away!" he warned. "Keep away!"

Shad stopped and stared. Kinlow was swaying on his feet. He looked tired, disheveled.

Once more Kinlow turned his back on Shad and began to move away. His limp made him move more slowly. Shad saw that he was aiming for the nearest house. Its roof was completely caved in, crushing the front door to half its normal size. Only one window remained intact. The porch roof was at such a slant that one end of it almost touched the ground. A picket fence reached up out of the drifting sand, looking like the fingers of a drowning man.

Twice Kinlow looked back. Each time Shad stopped, but when Kinlow went forward again, so did Shad. He was gaining on Kinlow.

Just as Kinlow reached the house he spun about, catching Shad completely by surprise. Seeing the pistol in Kinlow's hand, Shad hurled himself to the ground.

When nothing happened, he looked up. Kinlow had vanished.

Shad wasn't sure that Kinlow had gone into the deserted house. But he had to know. Otherwise, Kinlow might get away.

Slowly he came to his feet. Then he stood there, just waiting.

The day had grown brighter. A red dawn had begun to climb the sky.

"Kinlow!" cried Shad.

No answer.

Wishing there was something to hide behind, Shad began to edge forward cautiously. For the first time since he had begun to follow Kinlow, he felt frightened. He looked around, hoping that someone else might come.

No one.

He strained to listen. For the briefest second he thought he had heard something. He couldn't tell where the sound had come from. Inside the house, he thought. He wished it would come again. Nothing.

Again he looked back over his shoulder. No one was there. If he went to find Costello, Kinlow would certainly go and hide somewhere else. It was up to him to do something. He mustn't let Kinlow get away.

Shad took a few steps toward the house. Thirty feet from it he stopped, sucking some spit into his mouth, licking his lips, trying to decide how to proceed. If he stayed in front of the house, Kinlow might go out the back, might already have done so. If he went into the house, and Kinlow was there, he might shoot him. And then Shad realized that Kinlow could have shot him before. Why hadn't he? Maybe the gun wasn't loaded. Maybe he wouldn't use it, and he'd been bluffing all the time.

Shad took two more steps forward, paused, looked all around, then continued ahead a few more paces. He wished there would be another sound, anything, to show where Kinlow was.

Six feet from the doorway Shad stopped again. A new thought came to him. Maybe Kinlow *couldn't* do anything. Maybe he had hurt his leg badly. Maybe, when all that shooting was going on before, he had been wounded. Maybe he was lying inside the house, unable to move.

The gray insides of the house spilled out of the doorframe. Not a piece of wood was intact. Everything was broken or cracked. The tin roof curled in tight, rusty pieces.

Moving very carefully, Shad put a foot down on the ruined porch. A board creaked. Shad tried to see into the house. There seemed to be nothing but wreckage inside. He took another step.

"Stay right there!" The voice came from his left, from outside the house.

"Don't you move!" said Kinlow. Shad heard the man

move closer. "Now then," said Kinlow, "turn yourself around. Slowly, you hear?"

Shad did as he was told. Ten feet away from him stood Kinlow. He must have come around the corner of the house. He was holding his pistol, and he was pointing it right at Shad.

21

"ALL RIGHT, THEN," SAID KINLOW. "YOU COME ON toward me, now. Come here."

Shad looked at him. Kinlow's jacket was torn and wrinkled. His bow tie was askew. His stiff collar, pulled partly from his shirt, stuck out from his neck like a broken wing.

"I said *come here*," repeated Kinlow.

Shad, his heart pounding, inched forward.

Kinlow shifted away from the corner of the house, moving into the open space in front. With his free hand he beckoned Shad even closer.

When Shad was within a few feet of him, Kinlow held up his hand. "That's enough."

Shad stopped.

"Now then," said Kinlow. "You listen to me."

Shad stood mutely.

"I told you to keep away. You wouldn't. Now you're going to help me. I intend to get off this island. And having you with me is going to get me off. Do you understand me? Yes or no?"

Shad looked at the gun, wondering whether it was loaded.

"We're going to the dock," continued Kinlow. "You're going to walk right in front of me. And if anyone does anything to try and stop me, or you do anything different than I say, I'll kill you. I will. Do you understand *that*?"

Shad looked Kinlow full in the face. All he could feel was how much he hated him.

"You've done enough stupid things," Kinlow said savagely. "Don't you do any more. Now, do as I tell you. To the dock. Move out."

"No," said Shad, "I won't."

Color rose in Kinlow's face. For a moment he just stood there. Then he took a step forward. "You do as I tell you," he shouted. "Or I'll *make* you!"

Drawing close to Shad, he shifted the pistol from his right hand to his left, lowering it, and started to reach for Shad with his free hand. In that instant Shad leaped forward, hands balled into fists, striking at Kinlow.

Taken by surprise, Kinlow reeled, trying to bring the gun up again. But Shad was on him now, striking hard at his left hand. Shad felt a stroke of pain as he hit hard metal. The gun flipped away, tumbling through the air.

The momentum of his leap had made Shad fall to his knees. Kinlow, having stumbled, now desperately attempted to regain his balance. But Shad, moving first, and faster, sprang up and butted his head into Kinlow's stomach. Kinlow landed in a sitting position. Again Shad leaped. Kinlow tried to ward him off with wild swings of his arms. Shad struck harder, beating his fists against Kinlow. Kinlow finally managed to get his arms up between their bodies, and shoved Shad away.

Shad stumbled backward and landed on someting hard. He reached behind his back automatically to clear the thing away. It was the pistol. Shad whirled about and snatched at it, two fingers slipping through the trigger guard, inadvertently pulling the trigger. There was an explosion as the gun fired into the sand. The recoil drove Shad's hand into his own chest, momentarily taking his wind. His ears rang from the blast.

Kinlow had been trying frantically to get to his feet. At the sound of the gun, however, he froze, just long enough to let Shad recover. Gripping the pistol with both hands, Shad swung around and extended it in front of him, pointing right at Kinlow.

"Don't move!" he screamed.

Kinlow, seeing the pistol in Shad's hand, opened his mouth, closed it. Then he sank back onto the porch.

Shad got to his feet, looking from the gun to Kinlow, trying to steady himself, trying to keep from shaking, trying to decide what to do next.

Kinlow looked completely stunned. Slowly, unsteadily, he came to his feet, one hand clutching the broken porch railing for support, the other reaching out in front of him. "Give me that!" he croaked.

Shad, still holding the gun out, backed off.

"Did you hear me?" whispered Kinlow. "Give it to me!"

Shad remained motionless.

"I want that gun!" screamed Kinlow.

Shad didn't move. He told himself not to be scared of Kinlow, not to be scared of the gun. He had caught Kinlow. Now he was in charge.

"You're nothing!" cried Kinlow. "Less than nothing!" He took a deep breath. "You think you can stand up to me. Is that what you're thinking?" Suddenly he lunged forward, only to trip and fall to his knees in the sand.

Deftly, Shad danced backwards. He could feel himself growing stronger even as he could see Kinlow getting weaker.

Kinlow groped before him as if he were a blind man. "Give it to me!" Still on his knees, he surged forward again. Again Shad avoided him.

Kinlow struggled to his feet. Spit bubbled on his lips. He wiped it away hastily. "All right," he said, trying to summon up some measure of dignity. "What do you want? I'll give it to you. What is it? Ten dollars? Fifty? A hundred? What is it?"

Kinlow was pleading with him. With him, Shad Faherty! The expression on Kinlow's face reminded him of his parents' faces when they had come back that night, after Kinlow had threatened them. And right then, Shad knew what he wanted from Kinlow.

"Tell me what you want!" Kinlow cried again. "Is it a thousand?"

"I want you . . ." said Shad, ". . . I want you to go . . . to go to town."

Kinlow looked blankly at him. "What?"

"To my ma and dad," said Shad.

Kinlow frowned, as if he couldn't understand what Shad was saying. "Are you insane?" he asked. "Are you out of your mind?"

"That's what I want you to do," said Shad.

Kinlow looked about uncertainly, as if he might find some clue to Shad's meaning elsewhere. He pulled his bow tie off, looked at it, threw it down. "Why?" he asked. "What do you want that for?"

"To show them."

"Show them *what*?" He sounded exasperated.

"You."

"And if I don't . . . ?"

Shad, still using two hands, lifted the gun a little higher, pointing it right at Kinlow's face. "I'll . . . I'll shoot."

Kinlow looked at Shad. Again he lunged forward but

his leg twisted under him and he fell on the sand. Shad stepped back with ease.

Exhausted, panting, Kinlow didn't try to get up. He just shook his head.

"I want you to go to my parents," said Shad slowly, "and tell them . . . you won't hurt them, or my brother." He took a breath. "I want you to apologize for what you did. . . ."

Kinlow lifted his head and looked at Shad. *"Apologize?"*

"Yes."

"That all?"

Shad nodded.

"And then?"

"I don't care."

"You'll let me go?"

"I told you. I don't care."

Kinlow got to his feet. "You're stupid," he said. "Stupid." He tried to stuff his collar back into shape, set his jacket straight. He brushed sand from his sleeve. And he looked at Shad. The gun came up. Kinlow turned away and began to walk.

Shad followed.

22

THE SKY WAS PALE GRAY. FROM TIME TO TIME THE sun shone briefly, only to be quickly veiled by clouds. Gulls, catching the wind that came from the sea, swirled in great circles. Others, higher, floated motionless, riding the wind, only the tips of their wings moving. There was no sound, only the squish of Shad's and Kinlow's steps upon the sand.

Sometimes Kinlow stopped to rest his ankle. Each time he would partly turn about to glance at Shad. Shad would stop too, and would bring up the heavy gun.

"Stupid," Kinlow murmured once or twice. "Stupid as a pig." He limped as he walked.

In Shad's hands the pistol seemed to grow heavier and heavier. He was very tired, and with each step he took he felt more tired. He could feel wave after wave of tears rising within himself, like the ebb and flow of the tide. He didn't understand it, only knew that he mustn't give way to it.

The sun was well above the horizon when Shad and Kinlow came slowly along the beach toward the dock. Shad saw people on it. So did Kinlow.

Kinlow stopped.

"Go on," said Shad. His own voice sounded to him like a voice out of a dream.

"Stupid . . ." hissed Kinlow.

As they drew close to the dock, the people on it noticed them. Shad saw an arm lift and point them out. Someone broke from the crowd—Shad recognized him as Bennett—and lumbered toward the Front Street houses. He pounded on the Fahertys' door.

In moments the door opened and Mrs. Faherty ran out, quickly followed by Brian and Mr. Faherty. To Shad's surprise, Costello came out after them.

The two of them—Shad and Kinlow—now moved down Front Street, past the silent, staring islanders. They came up to where the Fahertys, the three of them, were standing close together. Costello stayed to one side, watching closely.

Shad and Kinlow stopped in front of the Fahertys.
Kinlow tried to stand straight.

"Say it," said Shad.

Kinlow brushed sand off his face. No one spoke. He lifted his chin, stretching his neck. He cleared his throat. "This . . . stupid . . . boy," he began, "insists that I say . . . say . . ." He turned red in the face. "Insists that I . . . say that . . . I am sorry. He wants me to apologize for having been . . . rude. . . ."

There was silence.

Suddenly Shad turned, stepped back, and with all his might hurled the gun. It arched into the air toward the bay, spinning as it went, and dropped into the water with a dead splash. A gull, startled, leaped into the air and flew off.

Kinlow, watching the gun fall, seemed to crumple, even as Costello took him by the arm and led him away.

Shad turned to his parents, to Brian. The three were standing side by side, Brian clinging to his mother's arm with both hands. They were all staring at Shad. He could sense their relief, their astonishment.

"We didn't know where you were," his father said. "He told us not to go look."

Shad nodded. But it was hard for him to think. The tiredness was rising up within him.

"Shad?" said Brian shyly.

"What?"

"Were . . . were you scared?"

"Scared enough."

"And you're all right now?" his mother asked.

Again Shad nodded. He just stood there, not knowing what to do, all but overwhelmed by a wave of dizziness that swept over him. Then the tide he had kept down for so long could no longer be contained. With a half-stagger, half-leap, he threw himself up against his parents. He could feel their arms, Brian's arms, hugging him, holding him. The tears came. "I did it," he said. "I did it."

AVI is the award-winning author of a dozen books for young readers, among them *Encounter at Easton,* winner of the 1981 Christopher Medal; *Man from the Sky,* an I.R.A. Children's Choice; and *Sometimes I Think I Hear My Name.* A librarian at Trenton State College, he often appears in schools and libraries throughout the country meeting, talking, and working with young people, as well as performing readings of his books. Avi lives in New Hope, Pennsylvania.